ALTERED AMERICA

Steampunk Stories
by Cat Rambo

Plunkett Press

Altered America

Copyright © 2016 by Cat Rambo and Plunkett Press

Cover design and book formatting
by Jennifer Williamson.

978-1-945477-05-8

Acknowledgments

I want to call out some of the editors who made particular stories the better for their attention. Liz Gorinsky did an amazing job on "Clockwork Fairies." Bryan Thomas Schmidt gave me insightful feedback on "Laurel Finch, Laurel Finch, Where Do You Wander?" Scott Andrews provided his usual meticulous edits on "Rappacini's Crow." Rachel Swirsky offered feedback on "Web of Blood and Iron," back when its title was still "Blue Train Blues (working title)." Wayne Rambo also heard multiple drafts, attended many readings, and listened to me brainstorm many, many points.

My students continue to be a primary source of inspiration. You guys know who you are and I love you all.

TABLE OF CONTENTS

Stories originally appeared as follows:

"Clockwork Fairies"—Tor.com, 2010.

*"Rare Pears and Greengages"—Eyes Like Sky and Coal and Moonlight,
Paper Golem Press, 2009.*

"Laurel Finch, Laurel Finch, Where Do You Wander?"—Patreon post, 2014.

"Memphis BBQ"—Airships and Automatons, 2015.

"Rappacini's Crow"—Beneath Ceaseless Skies, 2014.

"Her Windowed Eyes"—Patreon post, 2015.

"Snakes on a Train"—Patreon post, 2015.

"Web of Blood and Iron"—Patreon post, 2016.

"Ticktock Girl"—Cyberage Adventures, 2005.

"Seven Clockwork Angels"—Patreon post, 2016.

ALTERED AMERICA

Introduction

This collection, *Altered America: Steampunk Stories*, contains a steampunk alternate history that I've been writing stories in for a little under a decade, starting with the story "Rare Pears and Greengages." As I've written others, I've moved from England to America in order to bring in some of the rich complexity of its history. There is every intent to write at least one novel set in this world, though not till the Tabat Quartet is finished up.

This world differs from our own with the beginning of a fairy incursion in England in the mid 19th century, loosely chronicled in "Rare Pears and Greengages" and "Clockwork Fairies." As time passes, magic asserts a stronger and stronger presence. When Abraham Lincoln turns to necromancy to aid him in the Civil War, the North quickly wins and a period of industrialization and technological advancement begins, fueled in part by the discovery of phlogiston, a magical fluid capable of powering intelligent machinery. In the decades following its discovery, the 1880s and 90s see the opening of naval war with Japan over phlogiston, a war primarily fought along the west coast, as well as internal threat from a race of shapeshifting sorcerers of unknown origin.

This is the era in which most of the stories take place, including "Laurel Finch, Laurel Finch, Where Do You Wander?," "Memphis BBQ,"

"Rappacini's Crow," "Her Windowed Eyes, Her Chambered Heart," and "Snakes on a Train." The last two have an overlapping cast of characters, including Pinkerton agents Artemus West and Elspeth Sorehs.

In the early 1900s, vampires suddenly emerge as a power group, challenging the fairy hold on Great Britain and taking Eastern Europe entirely. They spread in influence rapidly throughout Europe, as chronicled in "Web of Blood and Iron." The story of their defeat remains to be written, but is on my docket for late 2016.

I have included two additional steampunk stories that fall into the right category but aren't entirely of the Altered America canon. "Ticktock Girl" was written in 2005 and originally appeared in *Cyberage Adventures*; it's a favorite of mine, combining superheroes and steampunk. "Seven Clockwork Angels, Dancing on a Pin" is a retelling of Sleeping Beauty that I wrote for a Fairypunk project and which originally appeared on my blog in early 2016.

As with other collections, I'll include afternotes that I hope provide additional flavor and enjoyment.

I'd like to thank my writing group, Horrific Miscue (both the Seattle branch and the national chapter) as well as many of my readers for feedback and appreciation of the stories, particularly those of you who helped fund the creation of these stories by supporting me on Patreon.

CLOCKWORK FAIRIES

MARY THE IRISH GIRL let me in when I knocked at the door in my post-services Sunday best, smelling of incense and evening fog. Gaslight flickered over the narrow hall. This was Southland's city house. His country estate provided his daughter, my affianced, plenty of space to pursue her studies and experiments.

It was comfortable enough here though. The mahogany banister's curve gleamed with beeswax polish, and a rosewood hat rack and umbrella stand squatted to my left.

I nodded to Mary, taking off my top hat. Snuff and baking butter mingled with my own pomade to battle the smell of steel and sulfur from below.

"Don't be startled, Mr. Claude, sir," Mary said, even as I asked, "Is your mistress in?"

Before I could speak further, a whir of creatures surrounded me.

At first I thought them American hummingbirds or large dragonflies. One hung poised before my eyes in a flutter of metallic skin and isinglass wings. Delicate gears spun in the wrist of a pinioned hand holding a needle-sharp sword. Desiree had created another marvel. Clockwork fairies, bee-winged, glittering like tinsel. Who would have dreamed such things, let alone make them real, except Desiree?

Mary chattered, "They're hers. They won't harm ye. Only burglars and the like."

She swatted at one that had come too close, its hair floating like candy-floss in the air. Mary had been with the Southland household for three years now and had grown accustomed to scientific marvels. "I'll tell her ladyship yer here."

She left. I eyed the fairies that hovered in the air around me. Despite Mary's assurance, I was not sure what they would do if I stepped forward. They were capable of independent movement in a way I had not witnessed before in clockwork creations.

Footsteps sounded downstairs, coming closer. Desiree appeared in the doorway that led to her basement workshop. She had been working. A pair of protective lenses goggled around her neck, and she wore gloves. Not the dainty kidskin gloves of fashionable women, but thick pig leather to shield her clever brown fingers from sparks. One clutched a brass oval studded with tiny buttons, almost glove-obscured.

Her skin and race made her almost as much an oddity in upper London society as the fairies. She was mine; I smiled at her.

"Claude," she said. Her eyes simmered with delight.

She clicked the device in her hand and the fairies swirled away, disappearing to God knows where. "I'm almost done. I'll meet you in the parlor in a few minutes. Go ahead and ring for tea."

❧

In the parlor, I took to the settee, and looked around. As always, the room was immaculate, filled with well-dusted knickknacks. Butterflies fluttered under two bell jars on the charcoal marble mantle, carved with lily of the valley. The room was well-composed: a sofa sat in graceful opposition with a pair of wing chairs. The only discordant note was sounded by the book shoved between two embroidered pillows on a chair's maroon velvet. I picked it up. *On the Origin Of Species*, by Charles Darwin.

I frowned and set it back down. Only last week, my minister had spoken out against this very book. I would have to speak to Desiree. I knew better than to forbid her to read it – but she should not discuss it in polite company or support its heretical notion that humans were related to animals, contrary to God's order, the Great Chain of Being.

Mary the Irish girl brought tea and sweet biscuits in a clatter of heels, muting when she reached the parlor carpet. I poured myself a cup, sniffing. Lapsang Oolong. Desiree's father had excellent taste in provisions.

The man himself appeared in the doorway. Lord Southland, one of London's notable titled eccentrics. His silk waistcoat was patterned with golden bees, as fashionable as my own undulating Oriental serpents.

"Ah, Stone," he said. He advanced to take a sesame seed biscuit, eyebrows bristling with hoary disapproval behind shilling-sized lenses. "You're here again."

"I came to visit Desiree," I replied, stressing the last word. I knew Lord Southland disapproved of me, although his antipathy puzzled me. If he hoped to marry off his mulatto daughter, I was his best prospect, being free of the prejudices others held.

With his wife's death, though, Southland had become irrational, taking up radical notions. So far Desiree had steered clear of them with my guidance, but I shuddered to think that she might become a Nonconformist or Suffragist. Still, I took care to be polite to Southland. If he cut Desiree from his will, the results would be disastrous.

"Of course he came to see me, Papa," Desiree said from the other doorway. She had removed her leather apron, revealing a gay pink cotton dress, sprigged with strawberry blossoms. She perched a decorous distance from me and poured her own tea, adding a hearty amount of milk.

"I've come to nag you again, Des," I teased.

A crease settled between her eyebrows. "Claude, is this about Lady Allsop's ball again?"

I leaned forward to capture her hand, its color deep against my own pale skin. "Desiree, to be accepted in society, you must make an effort now and then. If you are a success it will reflect well on me, and show that I have not taken you from the shelf, despite your age. Twenty-four is not so advanced that you are automatically an old maid, but people make assumptions. Appearing at the ball will be a major step towards dispelling those."

She removed her fingers from mine, the crease more pronounced. "I have told you, I am not the sort of woman that goes to balls."

"But you could be!" I told her. "Look at you, Desiree. You are as beautiful as any woman in London. A nonpareil. Dressed properly, you would take the City by storm."

"We have been over this before," she said. "I have no desire to expose myself to stares. My race makes me noteworthy, but it is not pleasant being a freak, Claude. Last week a child in the street wanted to rub my skin and see 'if the dirt would come off.' Can you not be happy with me as I am?"

"I am very happy with you as you are," I said. I could hear a sullen touch in my voice, but my feelings were understandable. "But you could be so much more!"

She stood. "Come," she said. "I will show you what I have been working on."

There would be no arguing with her, I could tell by the tone, but a touch of sulkiness might wear her down. Lord Southland glared at me as I bowed to him, but neither of us spoke.

In the workshop, a clockwork fairy sprawled on the table. Using a magnifying glass, Desiree showed me its delicate works, the mica flakes pieced together to form the wings.

"Where did you get the idea?" I asked.

"In Devonshire, an old woman spoke of seeing fairies. There was an interview with her in *The Strand*."

I snorted. "Old women are given to fancies."

Desiree shrugged, taking up a pick and using it to adjust the paper-thin wing hinge. "It made me think of how to create a flying creature. I chose to use bumblebees for my model, rather than the traditional butterfly wings. My fairies can resist strong winds and go where I wish them, according to the instructions I have laid into their 'brains,' which are tiny Babbage engines."

Desiree is interested in such things but spiritual matters are what I find engaging. She droned on but I cut her short. "Sometimes I think you don't love me."

She stopped. Her half-parted lips were like flower petals, an orchid's inner workings. "Why do you say that?"

"You don't understand my position," I said. "As a Dean, I must have a wife who is acceptable in society's eyes."

"This is about the ball again," she said. She made as though to touch my face, but I turned my head away, pretended to be examining the articulated form half-assembled on the table near me.

"Very well," she said. Her hand returned to her side. "I will go."

That week fled pell-mell. I went to a lecture series by John Newman and in the evenings I dined at my club and had excellent quail prepared in the French style. I went to the theater on two occasions, once to see Gilbert's "Robert the Devil" and again to see "How She Loves Him," by Boucicault. I stopped by Lord Southland's on three separate evenings.

Desiree had started on a mechanical cat. She took me into her workshop to look at it. A clockwork nightingale sang in the wicker cage hanging from the rafters, set in motion by our footsteps' vibration.

"It's still in the preliminary stages," she said. A brass skeleton lay disassembled on the table, but it was laid out so I could see the cat-to-be's shape. Mercury beads rolled in a white porcelain dish. A discarded spray of silver whiskers had been tossed in the coalscuttle.

I glanced around. "The Deanery has a basement," I said. "It houses our wine cellar and storerooms, but I have sent to have the front room cleaned and whitewashed for you."

Her teeth flashed as she smiled. Her breath smelled of licorice when I stole a kiss and I felt her skin's warmth against my hands. True, the room was not as fine as this, but she would improvise and makeshift, for she was a clever girl. And once she had started breeding, such fancies would fall away. Her inventions, her clever machines, were simply the maternal instinct thwarted. Once she had a child, she would find herself devoted to it. Our children would be handsome. And well provided for with the dowry she would bring.

When she went upstairs to speak to her father, I lingered in the workshop. I amused myself walking between the tables and shelves, examining at her work.

I paused beside what looked like a dress-form, a brass cylinder the size of a human torso. My cheeks flushed as I regarded it.

Shockingly, Desiree had given it the semblance of a maiden's bosom, a suggestion of curves whose immodesty appalled me. Headless, armless, legless, the torso stood affixed to three steel rods that culminated in a circular base as wide as an elephant's foot.

I reached out and touched my fingertips to its "shoulder." I trailed them down along the skin towards its chest. The oils from my fingers laid a faint trail behind them, wavering on the metal's gleam. It was how corrosion started, I knew. Given time, would the stains grow to verdigris, show how intimately I had touched Desiree's creation?

I buffed the marks away with a linen rag that lay on a nearby workbench. The stairs creaked beneath me in admonishment as I ascended them to join Desiree and her father. They had been arguing again. I heard her father say, "Blasted pedantic popinjay!" and Desiree say, "Oh Father," her tone coaxing and indulgent.

"You don't have to settle for such a man!"

"If I want to be part of society and not an outcast, I need the most proper of husbands! Claude and I will accommodate each other with time."

That had an ominous sound, but we would negotiate it later. They fell silent as I appeared. Southland's face was red with anger, Desiree's smile as bland as her mechanical cat licking cream.

On the night of Lady Allsop's ball, everyone notable was there. Silks and satins gleamed like colored waters, touched with flecks of light from cut gems. The air smelled of hothouse flowers and French scent. The orchestra played "Beautiful Bells" as the dancers glided in the waltz.

I do not entirely approve of such things as dancing, but society places demands on us. I was eager for the ton to place their seal of benison on my bride to be. I would dance twice with Desiree when she arrived, but for the most part I intended to stay on the sidelines, drinking lemonade. Still when a few partners pressed me, I gave in.

I know well that women find me alluring – no credit to anyone other than He who shaped me. But my calf shows to advantage in fine hose, to the point where at least one too-bold madam had called it shapely.

And I knew *very* well that it was my looks that initially attracted Desiree. Like all women, she is drawn to this world's baubles, not realizing their transient, mayfly nature. But with time, she had sounded my mind's depths and I flattered myself that it was what she found there that strengthened her attraction to me.

A woman I danced with let me know the Southlands had arrived. "Your fiancée, is she not?" she purred with a throaty sound. "I saw her arrive with her Papa, a half hour or so ago."

I made my excuses and went outside the Great Hall to pass through the refreshment line, looking for Desiree. I caught sight of her ahead of me, in the side hall's shadows, dark hair piled in an intricate mechanism atop her head. She paused beside a dusky silk curtain, speaking to another woman, blond-haired, blue-eyed.

From the back I could see Desiree's silk skirt: figured with gears, the teeth embroidered in red. I came up behind her and slid my hand through the crook of her elbow, drawing her close to show my pleasure at her presence there, despite her dress's outré nature.

I realized my mistake from the way the woman pulled herself away. She turned and I saw her clearly, no longer Desiree. Her hair held brownish red highlights, and her eyes were an icy, outraged green. The patterned cogs were Michelmas daises, the teeth ragged petals, scarlet on cream.

I stammered apologies, backed away as quickly as I could, bowing.

I searched through the crowds for Desiree and failed to find her. I looked around the punchbowl, through a salon of young misses waiting to be asked to dance, their mamas hovering nearby. Desiree had never been among their ranks. Her father had been indulgent, allowed her to skip so many social niceties. I sought her among the dancers and along the wall benches, where groups of men gossiped and women nattered among themselves.

Slipping outside into the starlit gardens, I found her there, scandalously alone with a man.

Pea gravel crunched under my boot heels as I approached, just in time to see him lean forward and take her hand. The night was cool on my outraged cheeks as I ran forward, pushing him away from her.

He staggered back, looking surprised. I had not seen him before: a dark Irishman with a narrow face and a nose like a knife blade. His black eyes were altogether too Byronic.

Sometimes you dislike a man at first sight; it was so for me. An expression that flashed over his face made me think he reciprocated the sentiment. He was, annoyingly enough, dressed impeccably, better than my own efforts, despite the Honiton lace at my throat.

Something wild in the cast of his features, the white flash of his throat, the enormous emerald on his hand, the way the moonlight glinted on his fingernails, made me think him something other than human, some besotted seraphim or an exotic nightmare born of hallucinogen or poison. A shiver worked its way down my back and spread its fingers to measure my ribs.

"Claude!" Desiree exclaimed, looking far from pleased at her rescue.

I ignored her, addressing the man. "You will not touch my fiancée again, sir. I am surprised at you, taking advantage of her in this fashion." I did not say it, but my reproach was aimed at Desiree as well, even though I knew she had not known better in her foolish, naïve youth.

"Lord Tyndall brought me out here to discuss my designs," Desiree retorted. "He had read the paper I published on the difficulties of imprinting tungsten."

I scoffed. "Indeed, he did his homework well in order to lure you out to compromise you."

Unnervingly, the man smiled at me. "I had no idea such an erudite work's author would turn out to be charming, sir, but the pleasure was unexpected. Having finished with that conversation, I was merely offering to demonstrate the art of palm reading to your lady. I picked up some small expertise in it in my homeland."

People were stirring in the nearest doorway, looking out to see what the loud conversation was.

Tyndall spoke to Desiree. "I did not get the chance to tell you, lady, your palm shows that you will take a long journey, soon."

His accent was thick. It was ridiculous for an educated man to speak with such a heavy brogue or to pretend to superstitious beliefs such as palmistry in order to lure women to him. But I stood down, not wishing to alienate the gathering crowd.

Lady Allsop peered from near the back, the frown on her face threatening future invitations. I bowed and took Desiree's arm, drawing it through my own. She resisted, then let me pull her into the house.

But she would not speak to me the rest of the evening despite the attendance I danced on her. In the carriage home, she relented, but only to upbraid me.

"I did as you asked," she hissed at me. "And it was as painful as I imagined, but you were not satisfied with that, but must take away the one interesting conversation I was able to find."

"Everyone loved you, how can you say such things?" I protested.

"Perhaps you were at a different ball than I," she said. "Did you not see Lady Worth turn away lest she contaminate herself speaking to a Negro? Or perhaps you did not overhear the sporting gentleman laying bets on what I would be like between the sheets?"

"Desiree!" I gasped, almost breathless at the shock of hearing such words from her innocent lips.

She turned away and did not speak to me again that night.

❦

The next day I came to call, bringing chocolates and flowers and a pretty opal ring. Opals were her favorite gem. But she sent Mary to tell me she was feeling unwell.

I started to leave in high dudgeon, but Lord Southland called to me. He was in his library, or so he called it, a small room that smelled of pipe tobacco and old leather, so close that one could barely breathe. On the wall hung a portrait of Desiree's mother by Robert Tait.

I studied it as he gathered his thoughts. I knew her mother had perished in childbirth along with Desiree's younger brother, only a few years after Lord Southland had returned with her from a trip to America. No one knew exactly where she had come from, but common gossip maintained that she had been a slave escaped from the southern portion of that barbarous place, that she had lived with the Cherokee for several years before the young Southland, on tour, encountered her in New Orleans. She was beautiful, although in an exotic, unsettling wise. Her dark hair hung to her waist, and the artist had chosen to paint it untamed, almost hiding her face behind it. Her dress's satin was the color of a yellow rose just opening.

She had never been accepted by society, but had been an exile, trapped in this house. That was part of the contract between Desiree and I; through me she would escape such a fate.

"Do you love my daughter, Claude?" Lord Southland asked. Rumor held that before his wife, he'd had other exotic pets: a tiger cub, a great hyacinth macaw that sang sea shanties, a bush-baby from Senegal. He was impious and had rejected the church, refusing to have Desiree baptized.

The question pained me, and I took care to show that in my tone. "Ever since I first met her, my lord."

"Ever since you met her, or ever since you learned she was a heiress?" He waved off my protestations. "I know, I know, such thoughts are unworthy. Still, I cannot help but wonder, Claude, if you did not think her an easy catch, given her circumstances. You are hardly the first suitor to make that mistake."

Desiree had other suitors? I was shocked but intrigued. I had never heard word of such.

"Still, the chit claims to love you." His look was contemptuous, and I stiffened my back under it. "It must be your looks alone, for you seem slow of mind to me."

I squared my chin. "You may disagree with your daughter's choice, but you raised her to speak her mind and choose for herself."

"I did." He tugged at a pearl-set waistcoat button. "And will you allow her the same luxury, once she is married?"

"Of course I will!" I said. "Within reason."

"As I feared. Very well, I will warn you, Claude. I will continue to attempt to dissuade her from this choice."

"What choice?" Desiree demanded as she entered. Her look at me was initially cold, but I smiled at her and she softened, as I knew she would. "Papa, are you beating this dead horse again?"

"Let me send you travelling," Lord Southland urged. "I will fund a trip to Italy, so you might see Leonardo's designs for yourself. Or America, where you can speak with other inventors."

"America?" she said. "Where they would take me to be a slave? Do you not read the papers, do you truly not know what danger I would be in there?"

"Desiree," he said. "For your mother's sake, and your own, all I want is your happiness."

"I will be an English Dean's wife and live at Oxford," she said. "Claude has promised me a workshop the equal of mine here."

Now was not, perhaps, the best time to correct that misapprehension, so I kept my mouth closed. Not that it mattered. Father and daughter had squared off like pugilists in the ring, and Desiree's fists were clenched as though to keep herself from aiming a blow at him.

He took an envelope from his vest pocket, ivory paper with an intricate seal. "I have had a letter inviting us to come shooting next week. The writer says he met you at Lady Allsop's. An Irish estate." He spared me a glance. "Claude is invited as well. If he comes too, will you accompany me? I would not have you wed without seeing other possibilities. And rumor holds the pheasant excellent in that region."

She gave me a questioning look and I nodded. Better to see Lord Southland assuaged, lest he put his foot down even more firmly. His difficulties were his own fault, I thought, for allowing his daughter too free a rein. Although it advantaged me more than a little, for I suspected her father's resistance only increased Desiree's interest in me.

I touched her elbow and saw her shoulders loosen. Southland kept glowering, but now at me. I smiled at him and laced my fingers through hers before drawing them up to press my lips to her knuckles, my eyes fixed on his. His jaw tautened.

⁂

When I returned home, I found a similar envelope awaiting me. His Lordship regretted the unfortunate occurrences at Lady Allsop's and hoped to extend an olive branch to myself and my "lovely fiancée."

Now that the moment was past, I regretted the assent I had given. But Southland would have written with his consent already, punctilious and prompt when he thought it might inconvenience me.

I decided to make the most of it. As Southland had noted, the shooting in Tyndall's district was rumored to be extraordinary. While the Lord –

was he one of the men that Southland reckoned a suitor? – would have the advantage in his home, the day I could not show up a country Irishman, no matter his title, would be the day I'd give up my position at Oxford. As for his inhuman aspect, it had been nothing more than a trick of the moonlight, coupled with my anger. It surprised me, how deep that rage stirred at the memory, even now, days later.

I turned the envelope over and examined the ostentatious seal. A pair of cats boxing with each other, paws upraised, circling a crown tipped with what looked like pointed spindles. A sweet smell came from the green wax.

I directed my valet to pack for the countryside. I would see this interloper driven away before Desiree even realized he was interested in her. Her naïveté gave me the edge – not that I needed it.

As we approached Lord Tyndall's castle, the countryside was verdant, the fall leaves just beginning to turn. The castle – for it was indeed a castle, albeit a small and shabby one – sat on a cliff's edge overlooking the Irish Sea, a romantic, wild vista that I feared might enthrall my impressionable fiancée.

I took care to point out the flaws in the countryside as we travelled up along the road: dull-appearing peasants and ill-tended cottages. I said I supposed it was most difficult to obtain supplies from London, given the distance and the road's rigors.

Desiree seemed to listen. Her father slouched in the opposite seat of the carriage and regarded me with heavy-lidded, inscrutable eyes.

There were a dozen other guests or so: a few Irish peers, and relatives of his Lordship, along with Lady Allsop and her husband. Everyone exclaimed over Desiree's exotic beauty and made enough fuss over her to render her speechless with discomfort. I hung back and did not rescue her. She would have to learn to cope with such attentions.

We settled into a daily routine, and Lord Southland and I both found the shooting excellent. I had never experienced such success at it before, in fact. It was as though the birds flew into my gun's path to sacrifice themselves. I had never experienced such a feeling of prowess before. The other men congratulated me, sometimes sullenly, sometimes with genuine comradeship. The women were invariably flattering, even Desiree, although it was evident that my skill surprised her.

It was heady, and though Tyndall came shooting with us less and less, I found myself able to overlook it. We dined well on the yield from our expeditions each day. Tyndall had an excellent cook, one who rivaled the best establishments. Her blanc-mange was airy as a cloud; her teacakes scented with cardamom and honey. A good cook, like a good woman, is a pearl beyond price. I resolved to woo her away before going.

Desiree was uninterested in shooting, which made me uneasy, but I was unable to resist the pull of the field. Like Desiree, Tyndall fancied himself a scientist, and like her, he had a mechanical talent. She had brought the case containing the clockwork fairies, and the two were working on refinements to the wings. Desiree suggested that the fairies could be used in place of courier pigeons, and despite the notion's impracticality, Tyndall supported it.

I asked what she was working on next.

"Something to delight you!" she said, her face glowing with anticipation. "Tyndall's workshop is so fine, I have been able to construct something that will amaze you when you see it." She laughed. "I think I will gift him with it when we leave. He has said so many times how clever he thinks my machines."

"And they are clever," I said. I touched the tips of the curls surrounding her face. They were stiff and unbending as corkscrews.

She pulled away. "My maid spends too much time dressing my hair for you to set it in disarray!" she said, but laughed to take the sting from the words.

I had found a staircase leading up from the main hall that had a nook suitable for reading. Always conscious of the necessity of keeping up, I had brought edifying and current works with me. One was *The Subjection of Women* by John Stuart Mill, a package of inflammatory claptrap.

Sitting in my refuge, I was about to put it down when a sentence made me realize even the falsest text might hold some grain of truth. The sentence read, "To understand one woman is not necessarily to understand any other woman."

I put the book aside but took that sentence with me, considering how it was true without being true. Certainly, every woman's personality was different, but there were commonalities at the heart of them all: a love of gossip, for instance. Concern with trivialities. An attraction to beauty.

Voices from below caught my attention. The stairway's acoustics were such that sounds carried clearly. It might have been designed for such a thing; I have encountered whispering galleries that bring a word from far away as close to one's ear as though the speaker stood there.

It was Desiree and Tyndall.

"I think a more durable metal, laid along the edge, will prevent warpage," she was saying.

"Your little fairies intrigue me," he said. "Where did you find the model?"

"In my head," she admitted. "I was reading a newspaper account and it made me wonder what such a creature would look like."

"You have never glimpsed a fairy in the wild?"

She laughed. "Oh, and dragons in the coal cellar? No, I have never been prone to flights of fancy."

"You think fairies only a romantic notion."

"I think people would like to believe in them, would like to believe in magic," she said. "Even I feel that temptation. But it is at heart a foolish idea."

"What if I told you I could take you to a place where you would see them, Desiree?" he purred. "Told you that true magic is wild beyond your imagining, that it will seize you, take you as though by storm?"

I was shocked that he would address her so familiarly. My indrawn breath betrayed me.

"Who's there?" he exclaimed, and came up the stairs swiftly enough that you would have thought he feared some intruder. At the sight of me, he scowled.

I, on the other hand, was stiff with indignation. He meant to lure my fiancée to some deserted spot under the pretext of seeing fairies. Perhaps he meant to compromise her to the point where she would be forced to marry him. Or perhaps the scoundrel meant to seduce her. I would have said these things, but Desiree's face behind him made me keep my tongue.

"Come to lunch, Stone," he said. "There is the usual cold pheasant. You have not lost your taste for it yet, I trust?"

"I find myself thinking that we should return to London soon," I said. Let him realize I had overheard his plotted seduction.

"Leave?" Desiree exclaimed. How could she be so foolish? Could she not see what Tyndall was up to? Was it possible she harbored romantic feelings for him? But the expression on her face was not thwarted lust. She liked speaking with him, I realized. It was nothing more than that.

Surely it was nothing more than that.

❦

A day later, I overheard another conversation, this time between Desiree and her father. I will not trouble myself to reproduce it here, for much of what Lord Southland said was misguided and wrong. He claimed that I was too dull for Desiree and said, absurdly, that she should find a man capable of providing her with intelligent conversation.

I would have interjected, but I had learned my lesson the previous day. Instead, I kept quiet and listened, knowing that Desiree would defend me as she had before.

But her protestations seemed half-hearted and, worse, she seemed to believe her father's words held some truth.

"You valued looks yourself," she said. "Was it not my mother's beauty that drew you to her?"

"At first, perhaps, but then I was taken by her manners, her bravery," Lord Southland said.

"Claude may not be intelligent," she said. "But he is respectable and well-rounded, in the manner of English education. And he has thought a great deal about spiritual matters."

"Spiritual matters!" her father exclaimed. "I thought I had brought you up better than to believe in the crutch that supports feeble minds in their mediocrity!"

Had he raised her as an atheist? I was appalled, but I knew I would be able to teach her, patiently and carefully, as befits a man with his wife.

"I want to believe in something other than science," she said, and I thrilled at the earnestness in her voice. "I want to believe in something wild and fierce and free, something that stands outside society."

Her theology was muddled, but she could learn. Her father's sound of disgust and frustration made me smile.

That evening we stood on the terrace overlooking the sea. I could not resist, but said, "Desiree, do you think we are well matched in mind?"

She hesitated, her indrawn breath a delicate whisper.

I did not mind. I knew I outstripped her, but I would reach down, lift her to new heights of thought, of philosophy. Some hold that the Negro race is a simpler structure, but Desiree had already proved that she could get her mind around such things as mathematics and mechanics. I would show her theology's wonders, the careful construction of a passage explicating God's glory. We would read Milton together, and other poetry that would elevate her soul.

I searched for proof of Tyndall's intentions, for signs that he was not a man of science, only pretending to be one in order to seduce my gullible bride to be. Desiree always thought the best of people. It was up to my more rigorous mind to show her her error.

In his study, a massive book lay on the table, its pages well-thumbed. I turned it to study the spine.

A chill ran through me and I pulled my hand away, as though from a coiled serpent. *King James's Daemonoligie.*

Using a handkerchief, I touched it, opened it. The words burned up at me:

This word of Sorcerie is a Latine worde, which is taken from casting of the lot, & therefore he that vseth it, is called Sortiarius à sorte.

Was Tyndall a sorcerer then? What unholy designs did he have on Desiree? This was far, far worse than I had imagined.

A cough sounded behind me. I dropped the page and spun.

Tyndall.

He had the gall to stand there, polite inquiry on his face.

"Some light reading, Stone?" he said.

I pointed at the book. My hand shook with emotion.

"No honest man has such a book in his library! What foul magics do you practice?"

"I have never claimed to be an honest man," he said dryly.

"Demon!" I hissed.

He shook his head. His tone was still polite, as though we spoke regarding the proper slicing of a breast of pheasant or the correct garnish for a trout.

"I have been called that before, on my visits to this land," he said. "But elf is more accurate."

"I know a demon when I see one! You admit you are not human! You want not just Desiree's body, but her soul!"

He snorted. "Her soul is her own. I want only her clever mind and machines, to entertain my Queen's court."

I gestured about myself. "Then this is all illusion!"

He shook his head. A smile lingered at the corners of his mouth, as though it pleased him to speak so straightly to me. "No, the real Lord Tyndall is…elsewhere. He will return when I am done, none the worse for the wear. Indeed, his fortunes will prosper as a result. As yours could."

"You mean to threaten me."

"I mean to say that the financial chains binding you to your fiancée could be replaced with other gold, of my own forging, as recompense."

"Desiree is more than gold to me," I said. "A good wife is a treasure. Fairy gold is said to melt away, or become dry leaves in the light of day."

"So you refuse to think of giving her up?" he said.

"She may not be much," I said. "Prideful and a little wanton, and overly obsessed with this world's trumperies. But she is mine, and I will have her, and the rich dowry that comes with her, and the inheritance that will befall her when her father dies."

"Do you love her?"

I hesitated too long. In the silence I heard the little gasp of betrayal behind me.

I turned.

Tears stood in her eyes before she fled.

She was nowhere to be found. No matter where I searched, even with the help of Tyndall's servants, who also looked for their absent lord, mysteriously vanished as well. But when I let myself into my chamber that night, I knew she had been there. A tang of oil and steel hung like dragon's breath in the air.

A shrouded figure stood beside the fireplace.

The note lay on my writing desk. Her handwriting was clear as copperplate.

It read: *Claude, I do not think we will suit. But I have left you something that will, I think, let you have the kind of woman you desire. She comes with my dowry – I will not need it where Tyndall is taking me. I wish you only the best, Claude. I hope you wish me that in turn. The key is on the mantle. Remember to wind her up every seventh day. -Desiree*

I pulled the cloth away. At first it looked like Desiree standing there, stiff and rigid, dressed in a gown of pale blue moiré that I recognized as the one she had worn to Lady Allsop's ball. But closer examination showed the skin was dyed cloth laid over a harder surface, the hair sewn onto the scalp. A hole nestled in her décolletage, just big enough to accommodate the brass key I retrieved from the fireplace.

I inserted the key and twisted it, hearing the ratcheting of the cogs and gears inside my clockwork bride, until her eyelids unshuttered and I stepped forward to take her in my arms.

As we waltzed, I wept. Wept for my Desiree – not just what I had thought she would be to me, but for what she had been, for her clever hands and heart and laughter, and that she had loved me as much as I had loved her. Tears fell to stain the silk bodice as I held her close, sky blue darkening to stormy. The fairies hung in a circle around us, left to dance by their former mistress. I wept, and we danced.

She danced very well indeed.

Afternotes:

"Clockwork Fairies" is an attempt to bring race into the conversation of steampunk at a time when it was severely lacking. Since then, a number of excellent steampunk works have appeared that manage not to be unrelentingly white, such as Nisi Shawl's *Everfair* and Jaymee Goh's *The Sea is Ours: Tales of Steampunk Asia*.

Rare Pears and Greengages

𝔊𝔒 Lily 𝔒𝔊

VIOLET IS ONE OF the halfies—mixed blood. Don't no one talk much about where they come from, mostly whores who took on too many Fair Folk. Means a nice purse for the lady, and then the fairies educate the baby and bring it back here. Why they don't stay in Fairyland, I don't know, but I know Violet don't call it Fairyland, and gets pissy-like if she hears me say that. It's the Old Country to her.

Violet sleeps in the same cold servants' room as me, where the wind whistles at night, like knives coming through the walls, but she don't seem to mind, not that nor eating cabbage and bone soup like me and Cook, nor not having no money of her own. Her wages goes to the King and Queen of the Old Country, she told me once.

Mr. Smith pays a lot for her because the nobs like maids and butlers with fairy blood. But he don't have to spend on her room and board, any more than mine, so she shares my room, up at the top of the stairs.

She comes to me after Mr. Smith has been up the stairs and gone again, leaving a shilling on the bed stand. It hurts, deep down inside, and I'm crying, not even worrying about saving the tears. It'd make him mad as thunder, seeing all them tears sliding down to soak into the blanket. Violet catches them, though, in the little bottle she wears around her neck. She whispers to me and hugs me and it's nice, so nice that I don't mind her taking my tears. Better her than Mr. Smith.

He don't come to her. I heard him talking to his friend, Mr. Ryan, about it. "Give me the creeps, that one," he said. "I think she doesn't bother breathing unless someone is looking at her."

Mr. Ryan laughed, nasty-like. "Doesn't matter so much between the sheets, does it?"

"Be like swivving a fish. That clammy. And worse—a dead fish, since they don't move."

He ain't always so picky. Sometimes he does a vampire girl down at the mill when he's been there inspecting it. I can tell—he comes back from those trips with a stink of old blood clinging on him. But he never comes to Violet.

When she first started a year ago, I said, "You're Violet and I'm Lily. A regular boo-kay. Like sisters." She looked at me blank as an empty window and I gave up on any visions of that right quick. But on these nights when she creeps into bed aside me and touches me with her cold fingers, it takes away all the bruises Mr. Smith left.

She whispers in my ear, "Maybe you'll have a baby, Lily" and the moist words are like ice water spilled down my spine. I'd lose my place if I did, sure as Sunday. I'd lose my place and no other respectable establishment'd have me.

"No," I whisper back. I fumble to light the candle end and find the bottle of vinegar and water. I try to wash all trace of him, all nasty slimy trace of him, off me while she watches. The wind shrieks and whistles like it was screaming No over and over, and it's cold, so cold.

"Maybe," she whispers again as I get back into bed. It makes me want to slap her face, ghost-white as a cellar mushroom. She never smiles, but sometimes there's a spark behind her eyes. A little spark, like when you set flame to paper, and don't know whether it'll glow and go out, or leap up in flames. Is Violet a glow or a leap? I have no idea, and so I don't say nothing, just pull the blanket around me.

I think about the lady next door, the foreign one, the one that looks so sad. What about her? Leap or glow? Violet tucks her pointed chin into my shoulder and lies against me, cold and solid as a stone. She wraps her skinny arms around me, but I don't feel her breathing.

Mela

The Colonel Sahib came to me and said come to England with me, and I will teach you how to read, and you can return someday and teach your people.

I came, but not to learn. I came because I could no longer bear the smell of the acacia trees, the way sunlight combed through the long grass, the grunts of the cheetahs chasing down an antelope. They all made me think about my son, grief like a spear in my side.

I would go to England and learn Iron and Progress and the death of the baby Jesus and how to forget. I made my goodbyes to the Elephant People and the Hyena People, but I did not tell my clan, the Lion People, what I was doing. They would know, they would catch word of it, but they did not approve, and pretended that the goodbye did not exist, as is our custom when there is something we do not want to say.

I came to London, where the air smells of smoke and despair. There were people like me, who walked as animals, the Colonel Sahib said, but only in one form—wolves. And in the twenty years he'd been in Africa, in Nakuru with me, they had become the pack leaders -- the upper crust, he called them.

"Demmed if I know just how they managed that, but they've made it clear enough they've no wish to associate with the likes of us, old girl." He patted my head awkwardly. "I had thought to find you more

company. But since the fairies came, everything's topsy-turvy. The streets are full of Fruit addicts."

I said I didn't mind and I didn't. My own people reminded me too much of my dead son, and other animals reminded me of my people. Now I go into the courtyard in the back of the house and sit smelling the frozen earth and watching the little sparrows flutter the complicated patterns of their wings and cock their heads, one side, then another, to examine the snowy gravel.

A gate in the garden wall leads next door. Originally the houses had been owned by a pair of brothers, the Colonel said, but they had moved on and now the gate between the houses was locked and curling plants grew along the bars in the summer, blue, odorless flowers kissing the space between them. I walk through the dead, icy grass and it leaves tear trails on my gown's hem, lines of black against silvery-gray, to look into the other garden.

Another woman sits there. Her hair is piled atop her head in a messy mass like a thorn-weaver's nest, and her clothing is white and filmy. The old Mem Sahib, the Colonel's wife, died in a garment like that after three years in Nakuru. A nightgown. This woman is alive, sitting humming to herself as though the sunlight were warm here, as though there were no wind or snow.

I do not make a sound, but she turns to me nonetheless. Her eyes are dreamy, a madwoman's or an addict's, or both.

"Who are you?" she says.

"My name is Layla." I stare at her through the bars.

She is a little dik-dik of a woman, but she shows no fear of me. She stands and comes over to the gate.

"You're not human," she says, looking at me. "One of them, one of the funny people, like the wolves or the fairies or the vampires, all come out of hiding."

Her breath smells of vanilla and her eyes are all pupil. She sways where she stands, and another woman darts out from a doorway, a maid, dressed in magpie black and white, to slide her arm around the first woman, supporting her.

"Leave me be, Lily," she says, pushing her away. "I'm human," she tells me. "I'm Arabella Smith. Why are you here?"

"I remind the Colonel Sahib of my homeland."

"And who reminds you of your homeland?" she demands, swaying again. The maid says something, but Mrs. Smith ignores her still. The maid is small and plain-faced and smells of sweat and soap and watery soup. Her hands are red and rough, and when she sees me looking at them, she pulls again at Mrs. Smith's sleeve.

"No one," I say. "I do not want to be reminded." A sparrow flutters too close and I slap a hand out, leaving only a smear of feathers and blood. Arabella Smith does not notice, but the maid does, and her eyes are wide as she looks at me.

Lily

We all run errands at the same time, or try to, the other housemaids and I. For one, it's safer. Men don't come looking so eager if they know they'll find you in a group, and anyhow the streets ain't safe. Betty knows a girl who got abducted, taken away into white slavery, and never seen again. I ask how she knows it was white slavery she was abducted to then. Tabitha says she knows for a fact witches come out at night and grab people, fly them up in the sky and drop them for the fun of it.

Betty gets cranky and says maybe it was white slavers or maybe it was witches but the important thing is that she got taken and no one ever saw her again.

And that's the main point, really, of going together. Gossiping and telling each other all the little bits -- whose mistress done what to who. Tabitha's not here one day and when I ask about her, no one will say nothing in front of the others. I get it out of them in whispers, crumbs at a time.

"She got in the family way."

"Missus found out and she were that angry."

"Said she'd have no doxies or children of sin in her house and threw her out."

"But Tabby had enough saved for coach fare back to Sussex. Said she'd keep house for her brother and her mum."

"Think her mum will let a disgraced woman in? I don't. I wouldn't."

At least she had that chance. What can a woman do if she has no family? Become a whore. That's the only door open to me if Violet's whispered words come true. "Maybe you'll have a little baby," she says in my head. Tears start to my eyes, but I fight them back. No sense wasting them.

Some women get hired to cry in the Weeperies. They say it's a cushy pull while it lasts, but you must cry on command, or be so soft that the Weepery can start you off by telling you sad stories or killing kittens. No one lasts long, though. They end up dry-eyed and hard-hearted as stones, while their tears get shipped off to Fairyland. The Old Country. How can it be old, when no one knew it existed until a few years ago?

I remember that day, when folks came running in to say one of the Parliament Members had said he was a fairy, and then suddenly it all came out, there was fairies an' werewolves and all sorts of creatures, all around us. They'd been around us all the time.

One of my errands today is the Fairy Market. It's down Threepenny Lane, near the river. Tents all jumbled and confused and everything glittering, glittering, shiny, the minute you come near. Glimmers of light, gone if you look straight at them. Ghosts of shapes. Goblins with their funny cat eyes, squinting against the sunlight.

I have two bottle of tears in my basket, and when I enter the market, the vendors swarm me, pulling at me to look here, look there, pinching me if I don't move quick enough to suit them.

They shout, "Rare pears and greengages, pomegranates full and fine, figs to fill your mouth, citrons from the South." I pick out two peaches, soft and juicy, warm as if they were full of fever, one for each tiny bottle.

At home, Mrs. Smith takes the peaches greedily and vanishes into her room. When she can't get fairy fruit, she drinks laudanum and vanilla, but the fruit is most to her liking. She'll be lost in dreams for days. Time enough to cry more bottles full, to buy her more fruit. I sniff my fingers, and smell the peaches, sweet and lush, and imagine their skin, soft and furry as mice.

❦ Mela ❦

Some afternoons, the dreamy-eyed, rumpled woman suns herself in the courtyard. I sit near the locked gate and tell her stories, the ones I whispered to my cub, long ago with the warm mud under our bellies and the blood of a fresh kill on our lips.

I tell her stories of crocodiles and storks, and the sinuous pythons that search through the acacia branches. I tell her how the little basilisks live on the insects and dormice they can stun, and how they dig their underground nests to lay clutches of eggs that may stay there in the dark and dirt for a decade or more before the eggs crack and their moist contents crawl out, bellies dragging in the dust, to make their way back to the safety of one of the big trees, its canopy grown up far past the depredations of elephant and giraffe.

Sometimes the maid Lily sits with her. The other one, the one that is part fairy, pays me no mind and I pay her none in return. I have seen her kind before, dealers in scraps, trying to buy the affection of their full-blooded kindred. She has her own thoughts, her own mysteries to contemplate. But the other, the human one, sits listening, wide-eyed. She thinks I am a great sorceress come from Africa. When I tell the story of my son, of how I nested him in a thorn-thicket every day when I hunted, to keep him from danger, she listens. She never asks what happens next and I do not tell her.

❦ Lily ❦

The first month my bleeding don't come and I tell myself it's because I don't eat much. Then it don't come again, and again.

I try to ask the other maids what they would do without letting on why. I know whores do something, something to make the baby go away, but I also know it's a sin. I don't know what to do.

Violet lies in my bed, and puts her hands on my stomach and sings. She brings me all her food, don't save so much as a scrap for herself, and so I let her touch my stomach. Her singing goes all through me, like something humming out from her hands.

"I can hide your growing belly," she whispers to me. "And when the baby is born, I can take it away where it will be happy. It'll only cost twelve pounds."

"The Missus will notice," I say. "Or Mr. Smith."

"I'll take care of them," she says, her eyes gleaming like candle flames while the wind shrieks. "And Cook won't say anything. Can you get the money?"

"Where will you take my baby?"

"To a place where they raise babies and educate them. Fine people run it, generous and wealthy. Your baby can learn to be something other than a servant."

I sell my best clothing and my mother's necklace, and that with all the shillings Mr. Smith has left beside the bed comes to a little under eleven pounds. Violet is angry – she rummages through my things, looking for something else to sell, but finds nothing. Finally I cry for her, and she catches the tears in her bottle, several spoonfuls worth, and smiles before bringing me a cup of water.

As the weeks pass, I cry more and more. Violet takes the tears away and comes back with fruit, knobby melons and glossy limes. She gives Cook something to put in Mr. Smith's soup, and he dreams his way through the days like the Missus. Cook doesn't like it much, but when Mrs. Smith is doped on fairy fruit, she gives Cook no trouble in the kitchen, and when she's not, she orders two puddings a night and changes her mind on the meat on a regular basis, right after Cook's just finished the marketing.

I grow bigger and bigger, I float my way through the house like a cloud, carried along by Violet's song. I think she gives me fruit as well—the weeks pass too quickly, too quickly, and then one nightmare of a night I dream my belly splits and I wake up in the middle of blood and soreness. Violet is wrapping up the baby in my coat.

"Give it to me," I say, but she holds it away.

"It'll just make you miserable later, trying to remember," she says. "I'm taking her to a nice lady, Mrs. Sucksby. She'll give her a good life." She gives me a glass of water, so sweet I know there must be fruit juice in it, just a spoonful or two to send me back to the coolness of the pillow and dreams of sleeping a thousand years, like Sleeping Beauty, with all them plants and thorns.

In the morning Violet and the baby are gone, but I am still sore. Downstairs everyone is cranky, but there is no fruit, and no tears in the house. I cannot cry no matter how much Mr. Smith raises his voice or hand. Finally he sends for the physician, who comes and leaves behind a blue glass bottle. More laudanum.

Mela

I smell the birth on the wind and it makes me restless. On the night my cubs were born, the rains were just starting. The clouds were low and lightning played over them as though the storm were thinking, dreaming. Then rain fell in sheets bending the grass flat, drops as warm as blood.

All my babies were born dead except my son. I was prepared for this. My people do not live long, and we are few. But he lived, and I washed him clean, there in the torrents of rain, my tongue and the warm water sluicing away the afterbirth.

The Elephant Women and the Hyena Women came to look at him and congratulate me, for their children are few as well. Three groups rule the lands where the acacia trees grow, the Elephants and the Hyenas and the Lions, because we walk most easily between the land of humans and the Real World. There are lesser beings there – we have fairies too, but they are little, malicious things, and rarely come down from the branches.

༄ Lily ༄

It's cold going to market without my coat. The other maids are stand-offish at first – Betty says they ain't seen me in months, and maybe that's true, judging by the differences in some of them. But they know what I need to find out – Miriam's heard of Mrs. Sucksby's.

"It's a baby farm."

"Whozzat?"

"They take the baby and board it for ya, or adopt it if you give 'em enough."

She gives the word "adopt" a nasty twist, so I say it. "Adopt?"

"One payment and they make sure you won't see your baby again. Got what they call a high mor-ta-li-ty rate." And she twists the words again like a knife. "That means the babies die."

Back home I go about my duties. Mr. Smith's angry, so angry.

"Where's Violet?" he snaps.

"I don't know, sir."

He scowls something fierce. "Have to replace her if she's run off." He reaches out and touches me, and the gentleness scares me more than the scowling. "Been a while, eh, Lily?"

"I'm having my woman time, sir," I say, very soft, looking at the floor. "Just started."

He ain't happy, but he goes off to examine the mill.

I slip out before dark, that gives me a head start. I know the address for Mrs. Sucksby. It's a part of town I never seen before, buildings leaning on each other for support like they was drunk, and everything dirty, so dirty.

The house hunches up between two others. A few lights on, but not many. I go round the back and almost walk into a woman sitting on the steps, but duck back afore she can spot me. She's a mangy old thing, sitting there enjoying the stars coming out, and finally she rises, gathering up her skirts, and goes off to the privy. I dart up the stairs and inside before she returns.

The pantry has a big cupboard under the sink. I dart under there and wait.

It may be been less than an hour I wait, but it seems like days. I keep hearing footsteps, and it don't seem like everyone is going to sleep like I'd hoped. Finally I crawl out and go up the back stairway to the second floor.

There's rooms and rooms full of babies up there. How will I know which is mine? But I spot her, wrapped up in my coat, on a cot with two others.

Footsteps sound, two pairs? Three? I duck under a cot just as they come in. All I can see is three pair of feet, one set of black ladies' boots, the others men's shoes.

"Take the ones against the west wall," the woman says. Light from the lantern one of them must be holding shines on the wooden floor, showing dust mice as big as kittens, and places where diapers have leaked. "That's a half-dozen disposed of, and not so many dying at once that anyone will notice."

"Do you think anyone really pays much attention to the death rate of bastard babies?" a man says.

"I think that we carry out this charade so no one will know they have been taken, and that we will play it out as fully as we have been directed," she says. Her voice is colder than any wind. It sounds like Violet's.

Her footsteps clack away, and I peek out enough to see what the men do. My baby is on the east wall, safe enough, but they pick up the other babies, and each time take a bundle out of the burlap sack one carries and lay it in the first baby's place.

The babies cry and whimper as they are picked up, but the taller man touches a finger to each forehead, and they still, snuffling themselves asleep. Arms full of babies, the two men leave.

I go over to see what they've put in place of the babies, but there are still babies there. One yawns and looks up at me. They look like any of the other children. I don't understand.

Voices, coming back up the stairs, and shouting, somehow they know I'm here. I grab my baby and one of the others, one of the new babies, and scramble out the window, out along the slanted roof. The old window frame slides back down after me.

It's cold on the roof but calmer than I expected, once I get over the fear that they'll figure out which way I went. Shouts come from the alleyway and I hear footsteps in the room underneath, but I sit where I am, in a nook between the chimney and the roof, with the coat wrapped around the three of us, while we get acquainted.

Mine has black hair, which I don't like, because it reminds me of Mr. Smith, and blue eyes, which I do like. The other baby isn't much to look at – brown hair, brown eyes. Its skin has a funny feel to it, like old leaves. It don't make a sound, just looks at me and reaches up a hand, tiny perfect fingers curling around my rough red one.

It's like me, this other baby – it doesn't know what to do. All three of us stay there, my baby asleep, the other baby watching me. The church clock, far away to the west, is chiming three when the witches find me.

Mela

You can hide a cub, but they will not stay hidden. You can tuck them among thorn branches, but they will not stay, and even when they do, death can come slithering down the trunk, a python to whom a cub is only a mouthful, a little mouthful, what the Mem Sahib called an appetizer when she served dinner to other English folk. When fever came, we thought the Colonel would go away after she had fallen, but he stayed, and little by little, we became friends, because we never spoke of our losses to one another.

Pythons eat cubs, and when they have, you cannot recover your baby, no matter how much you roar or moan. No matter how much you weep, even though lions never weep.

After we came here, a fairy came visiting, curious about me, about the Colonel. She told me what they could offer: fruit full of sweet hallucinations, combs and charms and little cantrips to keep a house clean or a man faithful.

And memories. They offer dreams and memories. But the price is high, too high and I have no coin with which to pay.

ༀ Lily ༁

Witches! When they swoop down, grabbing me, pulling me into the sky, I scream and almost drop my baby, but one of them grabs it as we whirl up in a rush of wind and stars.

"What's this then?" one demands. She looks like something out of a storybook: all long nose and beady eyes and hairy chin. I would have known her for a witch anywhere. "A baby!"

"Two of 'em, even," the other says. Her tone is regretful. "I don't want to drop er while she's carrying babies, Grizz. That's too wicked."

"Soft as pudding, you are, Sophie," Grizz scoffs. "Set her down on the clock tower, we'll find out what's going on. Mebbe we can take the babies and then drop her."

"I don't want no baby," the first says, but we are already tumbling through the sky, whirling like scraps of paper or feathers on the wind, to land on the narrow lip of the clock tower, gritty bricks nice and solid under my feet.

Grizz has my baby, and Sophie takes the other. She spits when she looks at it. "This ain't no real baby," she say. "It's a changeling, be dead before the day is through How'd you come by a fairy husk, girl?"

I tell them my story, holding onto the edge of the tower. Below us are London streets, and the faint distant lanterns of night watchmen.

The witches debate whether or not to drop me – "Keep the populace a little worried, after all, so they respect honest English witches," Grizz argues. Sophie reaches out for my hand and looks at the palm before she says something to Grizz, too quiet for me to hear, that persuades her.

I tried not to hear it, at any rate. I tried not to hear the words "not long for this world."

I have a plan. I make my way down the tower steps from the belfry with the babies. I know what to do. How to give my daughter a good life, the kind of life I never had. It all depends on the woman next door, the woman with the gleam of gold at her wrists and stories of a baby missing from her arms.

Mela

She comes in the very earliest moments of the morning, when the light is just starting to show its chill brilliance, little Lily with a bundle in her arms, to the back door.

When I open it, she stares up at me. There is fear in her face, but there is also desperation.

She says "Miss Mela, you lost your baby, didn't you?"

Satisfaction flares in her eyes when I nod, and she holds the bundle out to me.

"Here," she says. "You take her. You'll give her something better, eh?"

My paws twitch, but I don't reach out for the bundle.

She tries again. "Think of your son."

When I do, when I remember the perfection of his pudgy paws, of the needle-sharp kitten teeth, of the milk and flesh smell of him, I reach out. The baby is heavier than I remember.

"You'll take care of her, won't ya?" the maid says. The anxious morning sunlight reveals her features. "You'll give her a good life. Better than mine."

It is, as always, easier not to reply. That is the way of my People. So she turns away, reassured, when she should have listened to what I did not say.

Lily

After I've given her my baby, I go back to the attic and what I have there. The fairy baby and Mrs. Smith's big blue bottle. The baby looks at me with its dark eyes. Its skin looks older, withering.

I sing to it while everyone sleeps, down in the darkened house. I pretend it's my baby, that we will leave soon and go away to the country, to a little house, a little garden where there is sunshine and no soot. But even while I sing, I see it fading away.

Three drops, never more, never more, the doctor said. I put much more than that in the glass of water and drink it down.

On the bed, I curl up with the changeling, and pull the blanket and my coat around us in a nest of drowsy warmth. We lie there together, and I sing a song that sounds a little like Violet's and pretend it's my own baby there. The fairy baby doesn't breathe, although it watches me, its features fading, and slowly the darkness swallows me, and it, and we are gone.

Mela

I take the baby to a gate I know, a doorway that is watched by the fairies, and pay the watchmen there. They eye the infant in my arms with covetous looks, but they do not dare meddle with me. I take it to the Queen of the Old Country, and there I trade it for what she has for me: a tiny key that will unlock a drawer, a drawer full of sunshine and memories.

I slide the drawer open. It is narrow, one of many making up the brass-bound apothecary's chest. The drawer's thick walls make the inner compartment, lined with golden foil, smaller still.

The interior shimmers with a memory: mid-afternoon sunlight filtered through acacia leaves. My cub and I lay on the mudflats near the water, the chalky blue and gray water. The air smelled of the shift between rainy season and drought, when the sun-warmed mud begins to dry and curl at the edges. A big-headed baby baboon perched nearby, high in a yellow acacia's canopy, picking at the bark to make it bleed sap — a sweet, sugary whiff on the wind.

We watched it because the pair of flat-headed basilisks that spent their days quarreling over the division of the tree's many-branched territory were working together for once. They were creeping up from two sides, and between them, they might be its match, if the nearby mother didn't notice what was happening soon enough.

But she did, she does. The baby is saved, and the two basilisks driven off with furious shrieks. All is well. All is well.

My hand trembles on the drawer's knob. It wants to slide shut again, now that the last of its sunlight is gone. I keep it open as long as I can, but when my fingers' strength fades, it closes and cannot be opened again.

The Fairy Queen held a black-haired, blue-eyed baby in her lap and sang to it. And when she had finished her song, she took it downstairs, for servants are scarce in the Old Country, and it was time for this one's tenure to begin.

Afternotes:

This story was the byproduct of a separate effort that I was working on with Spencer Ellsworth. I was intrigued by the idea of fairies paying for human tears and an economy partially based on that. The title references Christina Rossetti's "Goblin Market," an allusion to the fairy fruit that Mrs. Smith is addicted to.

Mela the were-lioness is a product of overseas magic, and owes some of her existence to Rudyaard Kiplng, whose stories I steeped myself in as a young adult. She herself is addicted to another form of fairy magic: the illusion that her cub, killed by her carelessness, is still alive.

The witches came out of nowhere while I was writing the story and I kinda love their cheerful cackling demeanor. They seem like proper English witches and deserve their own story someday.

Memphis BBQ

A T THIS POINT IN the Memphis spring, wisteria overflowed the roadside ditches in frothy purple drifts. The dogwoods were in full bloom and the landscape looked idyllic.

Nonetheless, Postman Chaz McCartney was reasonably sure corpses moldered somewhere in those green-lit woods. With the Civil War less than a decade old, scars of war still marked this terrain where fighting had occurred. And Doc Lightning's bandit gang, which operated in a pirated zeppelin, had hit only two towns over a few days back, and were surely still in the area. He sniffed the air, steamy from last night's rainstorm coupled with the morning's hot press of sunlight.

But it wasn't the scent of death that met his nostrils. He smelled something else long before his horse got within sight of the Brown's cabin, hidden away among a tangle of redbud trees, wild blackberries, and kudzu. Barbecue, hot and spicy and greasy, a pepper-laden whiff that scraped the bottom of your lungs and set them tingling. He breathed in appreciatively, mouth watering, stomach sending up a grumble saying the biscuits and sawmill gravy he'd had for breakfast were long since dearly departed, and it was well past time to be sending in reinforcements.

It was almost enough to make him forget about Mandy. Almost. He'd pretended to himself that his errand didn't involve her or her mother's cooking, but it was getting along to lunchtime and he'd offend Ma by turning down the lunch that would inevitably be offered.

His horse snorted and jerked its head at the bit, full of spring-spangled impatience. He patted his mount's shoulder. "Steady on, Comet."

Forget about Mandy. But when he got closer, there she was, standing out front among what looked like a small crowd, shouting at her father. Not people, though, making up the crowd, but attempts at mechanical men, the kind her father Timothy Brown had been working on for three decades now, all of Mandy's life and then some. He'd raised his own lab assistant in the shape of his daughter.

Chaz couldn't catch what they were saying, now that Mandy had stopped shouting, but the way she was pointing at one of the mechanicals would seem to indicate the topic.

She and Timothy had identical expressions on their faces, puzzled and irritated and as though their fingers were itching to get at the root of the problem. The expression was more appealing on Mandy; the faint freckles on her nose and cheeks formed a perplexed constellation under her fine, gingery brows. Her father's hair had once been the same color, but gray was overtaking it, or more accurately had won that race a good decade ago.

"Still having trouble with that loobey-stuff?" Chaz asked, dismounting with a genial nod to the pair. Dr. Brown nodded back before returning to his contemplation of the mechanicals.

"Lubricant," Mandy said, not sparing him a smile. Her eyes studied the mechanical as though telepathically dissecting it. "Lessen you got something genuinely useful to say, Charles McCartney, you might as well get back up on Comet there."

Chaz scratched between his horse's ears, one of which flicked forward at mention of his name, before continuing to tether the reins to the porch rail. "Well now," he said, drawing the words out carelessly. "I reckon I would if I'd come to see either of you, but truth is, I'm here to talk to Miz Brown."

"Mother's in back, boiling," Mandy said. For the first time she looked at him, a little irritated and a little impatient and a little something else. His face, regarding her, was steady and placid. Her eyes were the first to drop. At that motion, he stirred. "Then I'll go find her. G'morning to you both."

He wanted to look back as he went around the side of the house, but he knew it'd be a tactical mistake. He'd been trying to get Mandy to warm up to him for years now, and she remained fixed on her work. His only consolation was that she dismissed her other suitors just as easily. He didn't mind that she'd taken up a profession or even to following Lady Suffrage. He didn't want a doormat of a woman. But she'd taken the words of that Susan B. Anthony to heart, swearing not to marry, to devote herself to science.

The thought soured his expression, and when he swung into sight, he was scowling.

Ma Brown was a burly woman, with farm-raised muscles, honed from chopping wood, birthing calves, and above all else, stirring one the kettles, famous through the countryside, that stood to her waist. In the depths of the one she was standing beside now, murky red fluid bubbled and popped.

"Mind you don't stand in the steam!" she snapped as Chaz ambled up. He sidestepped the steam hastily, expression easing as he peered into the kettle.

"What is that? You coming up with a new kind of barbecue?"

"Hot sauce. My cousin in the Territories sent seeds last year she got off a trader there, calls 'em phantom chilis. Hottest thing you ever tasted."

"Why do they call them phantom chilis?"

"Eat one and that's what you'll be." She smirked to herself. "Anyway, why are you back here talking to an old lady and not the one you're sweet one?"

"They're too busy figuring out their dilemma to be talking to the likes of me," Chaz said with a sudden grin.

"I already told 'em how to fix it, but they won't listen to me." Ma snorted. "Tim ain't never paid attention, but Mandy used to, at least."

"I came to see you, actually. You got a special delivery letter, so I'm special delivering it." He fished in the pockets of his coat, drawing out a thick vellum envelope.

She propped the long wooden spoon across an arc of the kettle in order to take the envelope, using the edge of a fingernail to slit it open. She squinted at it despite the sunshine blazing down over her shoulder.

"Want me to read it?" Chaz said. He was used to this exchange.

She handed it to him.

"Dear Ms. Brown, We regret to inform you of the death of your cousin Vaughn…"

She snatched the paper from him before he could read further. "Vaughn dead!" She crumpled it in her hand. "Good riddance to bad rubbish."

"Don't you want to read further? You might have some sort of inheritance coming."

"Ain't nothing I'd inherit from that man that I'd want."

Chaz had never seen her so angry. But before he could say anything, a shout from the front of the house caught his attention.

He turned around to answer that cry, but an upraised gun stopped him. Two men stood there with steam-pistols at the ready.

"What do you hellions want?" Ma exclaimed.

"Sssh, Ma," Chaz said. His eyes were fixed on the nearest steam-pistol's muzzle, a round hole deeper than oblivion. He could hear the gentle hissing of the guns, even over the crackle of first beside him. "These are Dr. Lightning's gang, if I'm not mistaken. Can I ask you fellas what business you have here?"

"Nothing a yer concern," the closest said. "But we're not the killing type unless pressed to it, as you've no doubt heard. So, if'n you'll lie down and let us undertake to tie you up, we'll do our business and begone so you can start working yourselves free."

"That's my daughter shouting round to the front." Ma squared her fists on her hips. "I ain't lying down till you promise no harm to her."

The bandits exchanged looks. "I'm afraid you're not in a bartering position, ma'am," the second said. "If you don't lay down, I'll shoot you in the foot, and if that don't do the trick, in the head to follow."

"Hold on now," Chaz said. But Ma was already in motion.

The bandits didn't expect the attack; that was what saved her. They weren't used to resistance, let alone from a woman. Their expressions wavered before hardening to the trigger-pulling stage and in that moment Chaz followed Ma's lead.

She plowed into one first, bowling him over and grappling for the gun. Her arms, covered with the brawn necessary to farm work, wrapped around him.

Chaz hit the second as his gun swung towards Ma, hugging him ferociously. This close, a steam-pistol could do a lot of damage, and he knew from the sound that both were well-primed. In a half hour, the chemical reaction powering them would be spent and they'd be useless until reloaded, but he didn't have that sort of time. Blue sky and ground flashed by as they rolled. He heard the pop and hiss of a shot, but couldn't see whether Ma or her opponent had been hit. He wasn't much used to fighting, but grim determination made up for lack of experience.

They crashed into the other combatants, who reeled towards the kettle.

Hands locked around each others' throats, Chaz and the bandit struggled. Breathing was hard now, and an agonizing stab as he tried to gasp for air told him he had at least one broken rib.

The other bandit screamed, yanking Chaz' opponent's attention sideways and Chaz let go in order to punch, a straight hard jab that snapped the man's head backwards and closed his eyes.

Chaz pulled himself to his feet. Pain banded his throat, constricting it, and his heartbeat drummed so loud in his ears that he could hear nothing else. Now he could see why the first bandit had screamed. The man's head had been shove d into the kettle and was submerged, a sticky red mass of barbecue roiling around his motionless shoulders. He was clearly dead, or else he would have reacted to the flames licking up his legs.

Ma crouched nearby, hands on her knees, watching him.

"Are you all right?" Chaz asked.

"For now." She rose, dusting off her hands and eyed the supine bandit. "That fellow out for the count, or should we dump him in too?"

Ounce for ounce, a woman could out-savage the hardest man, Chaz thought, but all he said was, "Leave him there, I reckon. Let's go check on the doc and Mandy."

But all they saw on the front porch were the motionless mechanicals.

"Took em," Ma said.

"But why?"

Ma's eyebrows knit in query. "Something to do with Dr. Lightning." She glanced down at the paper in her hand and started to speak, then reconsidered. She went on, "There's something we don't understand."

She looked towards the back of the house. "But I bet I know who can tell us."

They trussed the bandit in a sitting position, his back against a hitching post. The man's head hung limp at first. Ma roused him with a bucket of water, which brought him sputtering back into consciousness.

Chaz knelt beside him. "I ain't going to take up too much of your time," the postman said in his most reasonable tone. He jerked his head towards the kettle. They'd pulled the dead man away from the pot and extinguished the flames licking at his pants and boots, but he still lay in an unsavory, motionless heap. "All I'm saying is you can talk to me, or I can step aside and let Ma be the one getting answers from you."

Terror filled the man's face as Ma smiled meaningfully at him. "What do you want to know?"

"Your friends took the doc and his daughter. Why?"

"Yellow fever took Lightning, couple weeks ago. He was the only one who knew how everything worked, so we figgered we'd take us a new mechanic. Townsfolk said the girl was just as good as him; thought we'd use one to persuade the other."

Chaz' jaw went tight, but all he said, his voice mild, was, "And where are y'all holed up, that they'd be taking her to."

"The Pearlie slough," the man said.

Chaz rose. "Fair enough," he said. "I'm going to go get Comet and get him saddled up. Guess you can entertain him till I'm ready, Ma."

He didn't ask what she'd done when he returned, but he could see the bandit's threat had been removed for good.

"What are we going to do?" Ma said.

Chaz tilted his hat back on his head, rubbing at his brow.

"There ain't no room in this for you, Ma, as I see it. I've got to ride to Pearlie, fast enough to catch up with em before they get their ship fixed and float away."

"You're going to face down a pack of bandits by yourself?" she asked. "Don't be ridiculous. You'll need assistance." She pointed at the mechanicals.

He tried to make his tone patient. "Those ain't working. That's what the of them were arguing about."

"And I know that, son. As I was saying, I have some ideas on that."

At first he thought her insane, but she backed her theory up with hexological reasoning. The Law of Similarity. The Law of Contagion. And the fiery heat of the phantom chilis. It all boiled down to BBQ.

She used a fine sieve lined with cheesecloth to strain the steaming liquid into a clear glass jug before using a long thin funnel to drip it into the appropriate receptacle on each mechanical, talking all the way as she did. "Told you they'd regret not listening some day," she said. "They think if you don't have a string of letters after your name, your opinion's worth no more than a half-et ear of corn."

Chaz thought privately that perhaps they hadn't been too crazy if they'd rejected the notion of exposing their machines to a liquid composed primarily of vinegar and peppers.

Ma's sparker snapped, igniting the last mechanical. Like the others, it shuddered into motion, emitting oily whiffs of smoke, a red gleam shining in the bulbous glass lenses serving it as eyes, giving each a strange, bug-eyed appearance. She set each one into motion with one of the big brass toggles on each side. They trundled after her in a nosy mob as she came back to Chaz.

"That's a sight better," Ma said. "I'll get my hinny saddled up and we can be off."

"Hold on," said Chaz. "I don't remember anything about you going with me."

Ma eyed him. "You need me to operate the mechanicals."

"Whyfore?"

"They're voice controlled."

Chaz harrumphed, but nodded, shifting in his saddle. He glanced up at the relentless sun. "Let's go, then."

He kept Comet to a swift trot, but the horse, sensing his impatience, kept outpacing the mechanicals and Ma, so he'd have to wheel and wait for them.

They made an unlikely army. A rain barrel shaped one boasted four scythe like arms, the one beside it swinging three hammers of various size. A fragile-looking, attenuated one sported clippers and shears. Struggling valiantly to keep up, one dragged a box on wheels behind it, its many arms hugged to its side with the effort.

The bandits hadn't feared pursuit. They'd left a swathe of trampled bushes and cracked sapling, smelling of fresh new growth. As they left the road, Chaz slowed to a pace that allowed the mechanicals to keep up; Ma brought up the rear on her raw-boned, long-eared mount.

Chaz paused and held up a hand. The mechanicals clustered around him. Ma came up and he beckoned to her, leaning close in order to speak quietly. Comet eyed the hinny sideways; she returned the look with disinterest.

"We're coming up on the slough," he said, glancing down at the mud squelching around their mounts' hooves. "Keep back, Ma. I don't want to be worrying about you." He undid the strap on his holster, glancing down at his pistol to check it.

Ma gave him a reluctant nod. He crept forward, slapping away mosquitoes, hearing the squashy footsteps of the mechanicals, making him wonder if there was any actual point to stealth.

As it turned out, there was too much commotion in the bandit camp for anyone to notice him or the mechanicals.

The zeppelin dominated the center of the circle of lopsided, dun tents, sagging, hovering half-inflated in the air, ropes tethering it to circular metal objects on the ground. Everything was mud – each tent was set up on a platform of wood whose neat accordion folding showed a scientific nicety.

The oddest thing about the scene was the line of purple light, its origin unapparent, that surrounded the tents. Like the zeppelin, it hovered, but where the vast balloon was some twenty feet above the glistening puddles, the line lay a scant inch from the ground and water. Above it, sporadic sparks indicated some presence in the air. As he neared, Chaz realized the sparks were insects encountering some invisible barrier.

Mandy was squared off with half a dozen bandits. Hands on her hips, she stood over a slumped form that Chaz recognized as Dr. Brown. Chaz counted over the opponents. An older Negro man with a pistol, two blonde young men near enough in looks to be twins, currently not brandishing the pistols that rode holstered at their hips, an older white, a middle-aged China man, and a scowly black-bearded fellow who looked to be the leader, or making a try at it, at least.

Everyone was shouting.

"I tell you again, I won't cooperate until you bring him medical attention!" Mandy announced over a hubbub of "See here, Missy!," "You'll do as you're told if you know what's good for you!" and "Get that thing away from her!"

The last of those made Chaz note that Mandy brandished a small brass-plated device in her hand. She was as animated as Chaz had ever seen her, tendrils of strawberry-blonde hair escaping her usual tight bun to curl in the early spring sunlight.

"Stand down, boys, and let the lady have a little breathing room," Chaz said, ambling forward and speaking with much more nonchalance than he actually felt. He hoped that the mechanicals behind him would impress the bandits. Farm machinery was capable of doing damage – Chaz wouldn't have wanted to be hit by ol' Shovel-arms by any account, but still there was a certain absurdity about them that diminished the overall menace.

Everyone whirled, Mandy included.

All the faces held the identical surprise.

Mandy was the first to recover.

"I'm glad you're here," she said, holding herself poised as a parasol, "but your presence is unnecessary. These gentlemen and I are in the process of reaching an agreement."

"What sort of agreement?" Chaz glanced around. "I hear your ol' boss ain't feeling so well."

"Daid," a blonde twin said. The other elbowed him in the ribs.

"Do ya need tah tell im alla our business?"

"How'd he come to die?" Chaz queried. Most of his attention was on Mandy, but he was tracking every gun clutched in a hand, as well as the small machine Mandy held, a knobby, button-covered thing of brass and scarlet glass.

"That's aside the point," Black-beard snapped.

Chaz held up his hands in a placatory gesture. "I'm just trying to ascertain all the facts, son." He swatted at the back of his neck. "How about I come inside your circle, sit down, and we discuss how we can all part amiably?"

"Ain't going to be no amiable parting," the black man said. "You take the old fellah and we'll be taking the leddy."

"You don't need to worry she'll be subjected to no hankypanky," Black-beard added, glaring at the other. "We just need someone with the knowhow, now that we don't got the doc no more."

"Mandy," Chaz said. "Did you want to go with these gentlemen?"

The question was rhetorical. His fingers itched towards his gun. The denial would be his signal to move.

But she said, "Yes."

He blinked. His fingers froze. "Beg pardon?"

"I want to go with them." Her look was steady as a shot.

"Don't be ridiculous!" Ma snapped. She'd come up from behind as well. "You still got a passle of learning to do before you go off to become queen of the air pirates."

Mandy's chin titled upward. Stubbornness crept into her eyes. "I know plenty."

"Not where it matters. Trust your mama, I still got a few tricks up my sleeve." She jerked a thumb at the mechanicals.

Mandy blinked as though noticing them for the first time. "What are you using?"

"Never you mind!" Ma snapped, even as Chaz said, "Barbecue sauce."

"Barbecue sauce?" Incredulity pitched Mandy's voice even higher. "How...quaint."

"Doing the trick, ennit?" Ma gestured the mechanicals closer.

Chaz was aware of a gentle hissing, a sound that tugged at his attention. It had been doing on for some time now, he thought. Movement tugged his attention upward. The zeppelin held considerably more gas than it had before, its sides rounder, the ropes tethering it straining now.

The China Man intercepted his gaze and snapped something.

Everyone exploded into action.

Mandy pressed a brass button. With a snap, the ropes holding the zeppelin retracted, slithering back into their metallic casings. At the gesture, her father's head slumped down even further, then onto the ground fully as she released him. The mechanicals around Chaz clanked forward, but the bandits moved too swiftly. Black-beard grabbed Mandy about the waist, pulled her up the rope ladder with him, ascending even as his fellows swarmed after him.

Ma ran forward to claim her spouse. Chaz drew and aimed. But the ladder bobbed and jerked in the air, swaying as the zeppelin ascended, its engine now barking harshly.

He jumped. For a sickening second he thought he wouldn't make it, and then in an even more sickening moment, he realized he had and that he was moving upward as rapidly as the zeppelin. He spared a glance down and his stomach clenched. He set his jaw and began climbing, the rope fibers biting harshly into his hands. Up above, the bandits had climbed into the cabin and one was goggling down at him.

He expected with a certain fatality that they'd start shooting. But they let him haul himself upward until he emerged through the hatch and into the crowded cabin where Mandy stood with hands on her hips in a way that was indisputably her mother's. The air smelled musty and the interior was in bad shape, brass dials and trim overcome by verdigris.

"You get back off now, Chaz," she said. "I'm seizing my destiny. This used to be my second cousin Vaughn Lightning's airship and crew and now I'm taking over."

He gawped. "You're related to Doc Lightning?" He remembered the way Ma had snatched the letter away before he could read more. It made more sense now.

She nodded.

"But I came to rescue you," he said.

"You thought you'd come rescue me and I'd fall in your arms a-fluttering my eyelashes."

"That was among my hopes, yes." He swallowed hard, looking her straight in the eye. "I've loved you ever since I first saw you, Mandy Brown. I'd build you a home and your own laboratory and all the tubes and sparkmeters and gewgidgets your heart craved. I'd lay the moon at your feet, if you wanted."

Was that regret in her gaze? His heart leaped, only to be dashed by her next words.

"Sometimes," she said, and her voice was gentler than he'd every heard it, "sometimes that isn't enough, Chaz."

Under her direction, they set him down near the outskirts of Pearlie. By now the engine was purring like a cat that had been given its own cow for dairy purposes, the dull brass of the zeppelin's interior fittings was starting to shine, and the bandits looked like hopeful men rather than desperate ones. They lowered him down on a rope, and as he hung there, he stared up, willing Mandy to change her mind at the last minute, hoping until he saw her face vanish as the hatch slid closed.

Doc Brown was at the chirugeon's, Ma with him. She glanced up as Chaz entered, question in her eyes. When he shook his head and sat down beside her, she only said, "Timothy thinks my idea for the lubricant was mighty smart."

"Didn't say that exactly," Doc Brown murmured, although his eyes were closed. "Said it was unique."

"Much of the same," Ma said. She patted Chas's elbow. "You come round tomorrow, Chaz. Love may break your heart, but good barbecue'll build it back into operating shape."

He could only think of Mandy's eyes, filled with a pity that was worse than any other expression he could have seen. He looked at the sprig of wisteria someone had put in a little vase beside the sickbed, a touch of purple, delicate and light as air, and shook his head.

But Ma knew as she watched him. She might not have the book learning her husband and daughter did, but she knew there were things in life you could count on and things you couldn't. Love was in the latter category, but there would always be barbecue.

Afternotes:

I wrote "Memphis BBQ" in response to a story request received while I was having a wonderful time as Editor Guest of Honor at MidSouthCon. I went out for several wonderful meals there, and wanted to celebrate the occasion. The landscape is one I remember fondly.

The new Dr. Lightning's adventures are also due to be chronicled; she will meet up with a few other characters from the series.

Laurel Finch, Laurel Finch, Where Do You Wander?

JEMINA NOTICED THE VERY Small Person the moment the little girl entered the train. The child paused in the doorway to survey the car before glancing down at her ticket and then at the other half of the hard wooden bench, high-backed, its shellac peeling, that Jemina sat on. Jemina tucked the macrame bag beside her in with her elbow.

The child was one of the last passengers on, which was why Jemina had been hoping against hope to have the bench to herself, at least for part of the two day trip to Kansas City. The train began to roll forward, a hoot of steam from the engine, a bell clang from the caboose at the back of the train, the rumble underfoot making the little blonde girl pick her way with extra caution, balancing the small black suitcase in one hand against the pillowy cloth bag in the other.

She arrived mid-car beside Jemina and nodded at her as she struggled briefly to hoist her suitcase up before the elderly man across the aisle did it for her. She plumped the cloth bag in the corner between sidearm and back and sat down with a little noise of delight as she looked around. Catching herself at the noise, she blushed, fixed her gaze sternly forward as she folded her hands in her lap, and peeped at Jemina sidelong.

Jemina tried to imagine how she might appear. She knew herself thin but nicely dressed and pale-skinned. The lace at her throat was Bruges, the cross around her neck gold, the gloves on her hands white and clean. She looked like a school-teacher, she imagined, but not a particularly nice one. She felt her lips thin further at the thought.

The child, interpreting the flattening of Jemina's mouth for disapproval, fished in her bag and took out a small black bound Bible. She began to read.

"Oh, it's all right," Jemina said. Her boldness surprised her, but this was a child, after all. "I'm Jemina Iarainn and I'm a scientist, headed to work at the War Institute in Seattle. Who are you are and where are you going?"

The smile bestowed on her could have lit a room. The Bible slid back into the bag. "Oh thank goodness! I'm Laurel Finch and this is my very first train ride ever, up to Seattle too, and I was hoping I'd have an agreeable companion on my voyage."

She stumbled over the solemnity in the last words. Jemina said, "Trips are much, much nicer with someone to talk to. Where are you going in Seattle? To visit relatives?"

"To the Soldiers' Orphans' Home there," Laurel said, and her mouth drooped before she summoned her smile again. "I've been staying with my uncle for the last three years but he is traveling to China as an ambassador. It's all right, he'll come back for me, but in the meantime I'm to live there for a few years."

"Seattle is very nice," Jemina said. Her mind raced along the years before this child, living among orphans with no chance of adoption herself. Bleak, as bleak as any of Jemina's childhood years. "You will meet Princess

Angeline, Chief Seattle's daughter. She lives down near the market and is a real Indian princess."

"Do you know Seattle well?"

Jemina shook her head, then nodded. "My twin sister is out there already and she has been writing me long letters."

"Is she also a scientist?"

"She writes for the newspaper."

"Oh! Like Nellie Bly!" Laurel clapped her hands and Jemina sighed internally. A daredevil reporter was more exciting than a scientist, but she was the one constructing giant killing war machines, after all, even though she was not at liberty to talk about any of that.

The train was rattling along steadily by now, the countryside rolling past the windows as they left Baltimore behind. Someone towards the back of the car broke out a pipe, blue smoke creeping up to hang near the wooden ceiling, painted red with tiny stars speckled along it in a single long stripe. It was officially late morning now, and Jemina wished she'd been able to bring her tea with her.

"Have you always lived in Baltimore?" she asked Laurel.

The child nodded. "What about you?"

"I grew up in Connecticut, but I came to study at Johns Hopkins here."

"Were you there during the last war?"

Only three years back now, the great War between the States, which might have gone so differently if not for Lincoln's decision to treat with the Emperor of Haiti, to bring over necromancers who raised the dead, no matter which color of uniform they wore, to fight on the Northern side. And now they were at war with Europe and the alien forces that had appeared in those countries, the fairies, werewolves, and vampires.

"I was there and actually helped with the effort," Jemina said, trying not to puff up a little. She had worked side by side by the necromancers, learning as much as she could, pulling that knowledge into her own studies. It was why she was headed to the War Institute ther nowe. The last scientist-necromancer, McCormick, had died on a train like this one six months earlier. Jemina thought she would make it, but who knew? She played on a bigger game board than she ever had before.

To her disappointment, Laurel didn't ask what she'd done for the war. She realized that the child's parents must have died due to some military action. No wonder she didn't want to talk about it.

"I have a book," Laurel said. "Other than the Bible, I mean. Will you read it to me?"

"Surely you are old enough to read?"

Laurel sat up straight. "Of course I am!" She let herself relax. "But sometimes it's nice to hear it read and that way we can both enjoy it."

"What's the book?"

Laurel fished in her bag. "Alice's Adventures in Wonderland."

❦

As the train made its way along, they voyaged through the book, occasionally pausing to talk about its contents. Laurel confessed to missing the kitten she had left at her uncle's, which she had named Abraham Lincoln after the President. Her uncle's landlady had taken Abraham Lincoln, and had promised to write about his adventures.

At this point, Laurel's lip quivered to the point where Jemina hastened to tell stories of the entirely fictitious six kittens her own equally fictitious landlady had been hosting. In truth, Jemina had been living in the grey buildings of the East Coast's War Institute, and was not particularly looking forward to their counterpart on the West Coast. The Institute had promised her a handsome wage and an actual house to live in, though, near the campus where she'd be working.

Around noon, Jemina's stomach growled.

"I am going to the dining car," shea said.

"Oh. Have sandwiches. My uncle's landlady made them for me. They're not very nice," Laurel said with more honesty than tact.

"My treat," Jemina said.

She watched with amusement as Laurel worked her way through fried chicken, mashed potatoes, biscuits, and two helpings of apple pie chased down with a tumbler of milk. She ate tea and toast herself, the teabag left steeping in the hot water till it was tannin bitter, dark as oak-lemonade, and every sip sent caffeine singing through her nerves. It didn't matter if she indulged in stimulants here on the train; she wouldn't be able to sleep anyhow, only doze for four days till her destination.

"My cousin," Laurel announced as she mopped milk from her upper lip, "said many of these trains get attacked by werewolves."

"My cousin," Jemina said, leaning forward, "who is a Pinkerton agent, said that the kind of werewolves that attack these trains are very different than the kind that live in England."

The conversation had obviously not gone in the direction that Laurel had expected. She eyed Jemina. "How are they different?"

"They are shapeshifters, who can take on a number of different forms, wolves being only one of them."

Worry flashed on Laurel's face. "So someone here could be a werewolf?" she asked, looking around at the other diners.

"Probably not," Jemina said. "These cars are warded with silver." She indicated the top of the window. "See the little star? That's real silver and keeps out negative magics."

"You mean evil?"

Jemina shook her head. "There's not really such a thing as good and evil. There is, though, positive and negative. Negative magic drains things."

"What were the zombie soldiers that won the war?" Laurel said.

This was not territory in which Jemina had thought to wander, or which she found particularly hospitable. "It depends on which side you were on," she said.

Her mind flashed: *a zombie hand, pale nailed and blunt, groping out from the iron cage where it had been confined, in an early war experiment before they'd learned to tame them.*

She shoved the thought away before it went anyplace worse.

"Do you ever take off your gloves?" Laurel asked.

The directness of the question startled her. "No. I have a skin condition that I prefer to keep masked."

"Are you sick?"

"No!" she said, more sharply than she meant to. The teapot was silverplate, some of the luster worn away by use. She poured more tea into her cup and drizzled in cream, the white devoured by the darker liquid.

They ate in silence.

Finally, pushing back her plate and crossing knife and fork atop it, Jemina looked to the window as Laurel ate the last bite of pie. Outside were plains, great seas of long grass tipped with the purple fuzz of seeds, shifting in the afternoon light to ripple in waves. Far above in the relentlessly blue sky, a hawk hovered on outspread wings, dipping down, then riding an updraft higher in great swings like a broken pendulum.

The waiter appeared at her elbow.

"Everything to your satisfaction, ma'am?" He was an older black man, eyes deferential but solicitous of Laurel as he removed her plate. Jemina smiled at him and shook her head.

She folded her napkin in a neat quadrangle before rising and holding out a hand to Laurel.

"Shall we go back?"

❧

Each time they stepped on the swaying platform between the cars, Laurel paused. Jemina couldn't blame her. There was an exhilaration to the buffet of the air, the swing underfoot, the landscape flashing past.

They stopped outright on the last platform. Laurel clenched the railing, shoulder-height for her, with both hands and looked out. Her hair lashed in the wind like an Medusa's tangle.

"Will we see Indians?" she said.

"Quite probably"

"And buffalo?"

"Undoubtedly." Jemina had, as was her way, researched the trip well before embarking on it. She knew the distances between cities, and had the route plotted out on the map of the United States that hung in her head, colored with elementary school dyes, unfaded over the years.

Laurel took a deep breath of the wild air, sweet grass mingled with coal smoke, before reluctantly moving to the door.

Jemina stepped after her. They bnearly collided with the passenger coming out, who scowled at both of them, dividing the look and pronouncing them equally unsatisfactory. He was dressed in the Western style, with high-heeled boots, but a tuft of lace at his untanned neck, a dandy's puff that somehow set Jemina instantly against him.

She'd seen his kind during the experiments: wealthy merchants come to examine the way Lincoln proposed to win the war, aided by his Haitian allies, lending him their knowledge in order to keep their country from American meddling somewhere down the line. Men who examined the horrific with cold, calculating eyes while they smoked cigars and chatted about tax rates.

One of them had even asked about the possibility of zombie factory labor.

She'd stood with the President at one point, watching. He was a tall man, towering over her, dressed in a sooty black suit. His eyes were sunken, sleepless.

Perhaps they might have discussed the ethics of it all at another moment. But times had been desperate, and full of chaos and hard choices.

How did they test whether the Confederate dead would turn on their fellow but living Johnnies? They'd put them in together and at first Jemina had thought they meant to take out the living prisoners once the point had been proved and then she realized they had no intention of doing so. She'd turned her head, unwilling to watch, but she could hear screams and then worse sounds, thick, meaty sounds and gulping, and smell the hot tang of blood-

The man said, "Watch your step, little lady," and handed Laurel through the door. He was trying to impress her, Jemina decided, and she shook off his assisting hand as she followed Laurel.

Unexpectedly, he laughed as the door closed after them. Not an unkind laugh, but as though amused at the way she'd brushed past him. Her cheeks warmed as they made their way back to their seat.

They settled back in. The high-backed wooden bench lacked any cushioning, but Jemina rolled up her shawl and laid it against the wall for a pillow and let Laurel settle against her, a slight warmth and weight that was comforting, like a kitten resting on one's lap.

They stayed that way in silence for a little while, but the rumble of the train, the back and forth of other passengers did not make for rest.

Or so Jemina thought but she found herself soon enough in a thin sleep, dreaming of being awake. The back door of the train car opened and she turned back towards it in agonizingly slow motion, already knowing what she would see there: the encarmined teeth, the glazed eyes, the staggerstep of the broken boned.

They hadn't let her keep the charm they'd all worn during the experiments, the ones that warded off the undead. Those were expensive to manufacture and strictly regulated, because every soldier to enter the battlefield had to wear one or go down beneath the cold teeth belonging to his own side.

When she got to Seattle and began her work, they'd give her another. But here and now -- little to protect her -- she raises her hand as though to point a finger at the zombies coming so close she smells the carrion stink of them, the smell of rot that had made her eventually burn the clothes she'd worn when daily working with them...

She was awake.

She jolted upright, disturbing Laurel, who said something drowsily. Jemina stroked her hair with her right hand, settled the child back into her lap. Her heart still hammered uncomfortably.

She looked out the window into the darkness and could see only the reflection of the car's interior for a moment. Then as her eyes picked out detail, she saw the stars hanging far overhead, the blaze of the Milky Way, a curdle of starlight spilling over the plains that rolled out as far as the eye could see.

Chuggadrum, chuggadrum, the sound of the wheels underfoot, the everpresent vibration working its way through her body as they hurtled through the night towards Seattle.

They'd promised her a laboratory of her own. A budget. Assistants.

Things she could do without interference. That was worth a lot, for a woman in a field that held so few other of her sex.

"I have nightmares sometimes too," Laurel said.

Jemina's hand sleeked over the curve of Laurel's skull, cloth sliding over glossy hair.

"We all do."

"What are yours about?"

"The war. What about yours?"

Laurel lay silent so long that Jemina thought she had gone back to sleep. But finally she said, "How my parents died."

Jemina's fingers stilled. She waited.

"We were in the house and they came," Lauren said. "My uncle said they were supposed to stay on the battlefield and no one knew they went the wrong way."

Her voice was subdued, thoughtful.

"Mama was upstairs singing to me. She sang a song she made up, 'Laurel Finch, Laurel Finch, where do you wander?" She had a pretty voice, Mama did. It would have been all right, but papa heard them at the door and he went and opened it. That was how they got in."

Jemina saw it in her mind's eye, despite her attempt to force it away: the man mowed down, devoured with that frightening completeness that zombies had, before they moved on to the rest of the house...the song faltering, the mother trying to hide her child from the ravenous attack.

"How did you get away?" she asked.

"I jumped out the window and ran. I tried to get my little brother first, but it was too late, so I ran."

"Your brother?"

"He was just a baby. He couldn't run." Laurel moved her head in slow negation. "Too late."

Jemina closed her eyes, feeling the story wrenching at her heart.

These things happened in war. They were sad, yes, but unavoidable.

The wheels screeched as the train slowed. Both of them sat up to look out the window.

"Who are those men?" Laurel asked.

"I don't know." But she did, given the fact that the group had bandanas tugged up around their faces, and that many had pistols or Springfield rifles in their hands.

"They're bandits!" Laurel's voice was excited.

"Yes," Jemina admitted.

They waited. Around them, everyone was abuzz, but stayed in their seats. The front door of the car swung open and two men entered, both holding pistols, red cloth masking everything except their eyes. Both were hatless, stringy hair matted with dust and sweat.

"We're looking for a fellow name of J. Iarainn," one called to the car at large. "You here, Mr. Iarainn? If not, I'm going to start shooting people one by one, cause according to the manifest, you're in this car."

Jemina held up a hand. "I am Jemina Iarainn."

Her gender astonished them. They squinted at her before exchanging glances.

"You headed to Seattle and the War Institute to work? Some kinda necromancery?"

"Yes to Seattle, yes to the War Institute. No to necromancy. I hold joint degrees in medicine and engineering, specializing in artificial limbs."

Exasperation kept her calm. Why should these dunces not believe a female scientist could exist? And necromancy -- she was, by far, tired of that label. She worked with devices for the products of such technology, but she wielded the forces of science, of steam and electricity and phlogiston.

"Right then." The speaker had made up his mind. "You come with me and my friend is going to talk to these nice people and collect their cash."

"Pretty little girl," the other said, smiling at Laurel, a smile that chilled the base of Jemina's spine.

"She comes with me," she said, putting her right hand on Laurel's shoulder.

"She your daughter?"

"Yes," she said. Laurel's hand reached up to steal into hers, trembling.

"Wait," someone said from behind them.

Jemina gathered Laurel behind her skirts, watching the gun rather than looking to the voice. She recognized it nonetheless: the dandy they'd met on the platform.

"I'm Miz Iarainn's guard, escorting her to Seattle," he said.

This time, surprise at the claim prompted Jemina to look around. He had a gun in his hand as well but his posture was easy, relaxed, where the bandits' was not.

"We don't need you interfering," one bandit said.

"All I'm going to do is follow along and make sure Miz Iarainn's visit goes well," he said. "You taking her somewhere, I'll just meander thataway with you." He cast a glance at Laurel. "Do some babysitting if need be of Miz Iarainn's...daughter." He winked at Jemina.

At least it was someone else for the guns to point at, she reflected.

They exited the train in a small group, Jemina and Laurel preceding dandy and first bandit while the second bandit remained behind.

Once off the train, she could see what had stopped it. A wagon had been driven across the tracks. The cowcatcher was within inches of it. If they'd been going any faster, there would have been a crash.

Another dozen men stood with the horses. The engineer and conductor both knelt in the long grass with their fingers laced behind their heads. Other men came from the other cars, most of them carrying canvas sacks that sagged with weight.

The bandit walked up to a man who was unmasked, who sat on a spotted horse.

"Boss..." he said hesitantly.

The man on horseback looked down. His brows knitted. "This the fellow?" he asked. "You brung his family along? What for?"

"The lady's the fellow," the bandit said. "T'other fellow says he's her guard."

"That so?" the unmasked man said. He drew his revolver and pointed it at the dandy's head. "And why do you think she needs a guard?"

The dandy smirked. His gun remained trained on the bandit that had brought them. "I'm just..." he began.

The other man's gun barked. The dandy's eyes rolled up in his head and he slumped to the ground. Laurel shrieked; Jemina's hands tightened on her shoulders, but she did not react otherwise.

The leader studied her. "You're the scientist?"

"I am." The levelness of her voice pleased her. "You're the boss here?"

He laughed, a whip crack of a sound. "No. You'll meet him, back at the camp." He whistled shrilly. "Saddle up, boys."

❧

It felt as though they rode for hours through the relentlessly flat landscape. As they did so, Jemina realized there were folds and wrinkles to the land, and once or twice a distant smudge of trees marking, she presumed, a water source.

They came on the camp in one of these folds, so abruptly it barely registered before they were stumbling down a slope and being hauled down off the horses.

Jemina's hands had been tied in front of her. She wiped at her face, leaving streaks of dust on the crumpled white gloves. Laurel pressed close.

"Come on," the man who'd shot the dandy said.

He led them through a cluster of tents. It was almost noon now, and the sun pushed down with impatient heat. When they entered the largest tent, it was cooler there, but there was an undertone to the air that Jemina recognized, a sour sweet smell of carrion.

She was not surprised to see the creature that sat in a makeshift throne made of powder kegs and chests. A ghoul. She'd seen a few during the war, come to feast after battles, but they had been easy enough to drive away. Now here was one that had co-opted humans to serve it. Judging from the chest that spilled out currency and gold to one side, it had no problem with finding its hirelings.

The face was red-eyed, the nose too broad, the cheeks too thick to seem human. The rasping voice seemed equally monstrous.

"You are the one traveling to the War Institute? We were given word you were coming."

"Yes," Jemina said cautiously.

"You are a necromancer then?"

She shook her head. This again. "No. I am an engineer specializing in artificial limbs. I'm going to Seattle to work with the War Institute on a new effort."

The red eyes studied her. "What sort of effort?"

"I'm not at liberty to say." But really, how hard was it to guess? Zombies plus specialized limbs. Super soldiers.

The lips pursed in disappointment. "I wanted a necromancer. An engineer is no use to me." It flapped a hand. "Take them to a cell. I'll eat them later."

The bandit that escorted them seemed nonchalant, smoking a hand-rolled cigarette and refusing to reply to any of Jemina's sallies.

"He's going to eat us," Laurel said and burst into tears.

Jemina shook her head. "He's not going to have the chance," she said.

"Why not?"

They were locked in but alone. Jemina felt through her pocket for chalk. "Because I'm not a necromancer, but I am something better."

"What's that?"

"They call me a necromantic engineer."

⚶

When the explosion came, Jemina scrambled to her feet. Out of the cloud of smoke, a figure stumbled.

Laurel screamed. "A zombie!"

"A summoned zombie," Jemina said. She felt tired and old. Her forearm throbbed where she'd scratched it to get the necessary blood. "It lit the throne. Foolish to sit on a powder keg if you don't expect it to blow up on you."

Step by staggering step, the dead man came forward, hand gripping the keys, stuck out in front of him. When they extended into the cell Jemina reached out to take them. As she did, they locked eyes.

"Be at peace," she said, and watched as the body fell.

She unlocked the cell. "Come on. We'll see if there are any horses. Even if there's survivors, they'll be busy enough that no one should stop us."

"You would think so," a voice said.

The ghoul. It stood there, scorched but intact. "Foolish woman," it said. "Now what will you do?"

"This," Jemina said, pointing her left hand at him. The white glove fell into scraps as the bullet left the hollow chamber of her finger, revealing the brass and copper limb underneath, shining as he gaped.

"Silver bullet," Jemina told him. Stepping over, she rifled through his pockets, removing valuables.

"Are we going to Seattle now?" Laurel asked.

"No," Jemina said, filling her pockets with what she'd gleaned. "I'm done with all this."

"Then where will we go?"

"Anywhere," Jemina said and held out her human hand.

After all, this was a wild new world, even if parts of it were war-wracked. This was the Mechanical age, and its practitioners would be welcome in almost any town.

"Laurel Finch, Laurel Finch, where will we wander?" she said.

Laurel took her hand.

Afternotes:

This story came from an image of a small, scared girl getting on a train. It's the same line that Elspeth and Artemus travel on, a story later, as they head towards events in Seattle, and Jemina will be visiting the locale of "Rappacini's Crow" in an adventure yet to come.

Bryan Thomas Schmidt's comments on the story's ending were very helpful; the story is the better for his insight.

Snakes on a Train

E LSPETH FOLDED HER HANDS in her lap, trying to keep her brows from knitting. She hated trains.

They were dirty, with bits of smut and coal blown back from the massive brass and aluminum steam engine pulling them along, and engrimed by successions of previous passengers.

They were noisy, from the engine's howl to the screech of the never-sufficiently-greased axles as they rocketed along the steel rails with their steady pocketa-pocketa-pocketa chug seeping up through the swaying floor.

And they were oppressively full of people, all thinking things, all pressing down on her Sensitive's mind, making her shrink down into the hard wooden seat as though the haze of thoughts hung like coal-smoke in the air and if she sank low enough, she'd avoid it.

She glanced over at her fellow Pinkerton agent, who returned her look with his own slightly quizzical if impersonal gaze. All of the curiosity of their fellow passengers was directed at him, perhaps the first mechanical being they'd ever seen, with silver and brass skin and curly hair, eyebrows, and moustache of gilded wire.

"They shouldn't be keeping us back here," she said for the third time in as many minutes. "If we're his assigned bodyguards, they should let us up to inspect his compartment."

"The porter said he'd tell them we were here," Artemus said in precisely the same tone he'd used the first two times he'd said these words.

Elspeth sighed. Even as she did so, the porter entered the car and signaled to them.

"You go up two cars," he said, and pointed.

They made their way through the creak and sway of a car identical to theirs, then the narrower corridors of a sleeper car. Artemus knocked on a doorway and they poked their heads into a compartment where their package stood with his daughter.

That package, one Joshua McCormick, was a short, brawny little man who held himself with a terrier's alertness. His hair had retreated from the majority of his freckled brown scalp, but still tufted over his ears, which supported the frames of two brass-rimmed spectacles, the left one wider rimmed and more elaborate than the right. His daughter Belinda was unpacking McCormick's trunk with an assistant's familiarity. As Elspeth watched, she unfolded a trunk and set it against the wall so the myriad of tiny drawers and bottles it held were accessible, held in with straps against the train's constant jostle.

Artemus said, "Sir, do you intend to undertake experiments here on the train?"

Professor McCormick shook his head, brows knitting. He folded his arms and glared over at his daughter. "Belinda. It's true. I won't be doing much on the train. If you unpack all of that, it'll just be in our way."

The daughter's stiff shoulders told Elspeth of the daughter's resentment. But she relaxed as the lack of emotions battering against her mind confirmed what they'd been told was a the case: the girl was a psychic null, whose thoughts could not be sensed and who would be able to withstand most mental powers.

It was one of the things she valued about Artemus—the absence of thoughts twitching her one way or another. She was looking forward to spending time with Belinda McCormick, if not her father's roil of pride and greed and anger.

The Professor wheeled to address Artemus just as roughly. "I've told your superiors that your presence is unnecessary."

Another thing Elspeth appreciated about Artemus as his ability to keep his voice modulated where Elspeth knew irritation would have wasp-whined her own tone. "I'm sure that's true, sir. But there are definite and established dangers and not every train headed from Baltimore to Seattle has made it to its destination. Your expertise is important to the War Effort, and so we've been hired to make sure you get there as quickly and smoothly as you can. If you relax and let us proceed in our efforts, you'll find the journey goes quickly and with a minimum of fuss."

The Professor's attention swiveled ponderously between the two of them.

"What sort of dangers have presented themselves?" he demanded, brows beetling in suspicion. "Not the made-up panics from the papers, mind you. The *real* dangers."

"There have been instances of werewolves, which were responsible for the recent derailment of a train. And lizard-wizards, more than one."

"Snakes?"

"That is the name some call them by, yes." Artemus's voice remained glassy smooth. "We have twelve hours before we reach Kansas City. I'd suggest you get settled and then go to sleep as early as possible. I'm told many people find the rattle of the wheels soporific."

McCormick looked offended by the reminder of Artemus's mechanical state. "And what are you? Is someone operating you remotely?"

"I'm automatous. This is my partner, Elspeth Sorehs."

"A Hasidic." The Professor's eyes assessed Elspeth frankly, and his thoughts pawed at her. She forced down her reaction. He couldn't know that what he was thinking was offensive. That was what almost all men did, thought in terms of what they would have been able to see if the fabric and stays were stripped away, how cupable her breasts, her thickly fleeced her thighs, this one no less than any other. She looked down at the floor.

"You will be in the cubby across the way?" the Professor addressed her.

"I will," she said. "Mr. West..." She stressed the honorific and surname in a way that ratcheted the older man's brows further upward. "Mr. West will be watching the corridor outside your cubby. He is unsleeping." It would be a rare creature indeed that made its way past Artemus.

"The train will serve a late dinner in forty-five minutes," the Professor said. "You will join us." He turned and went back into the room where his daughter stood.

Elspeth rolled her eyes at Artemus. She stuck her head in their own compartment, eying the tiny bunks.

"Well, it's snug," she said. She sniffed at herself, ruefully noticing the sour tang to the fabric. That was the worst part of traveling, the lack of bathing facilities.

"There'll be a bathhouse in Kansas City, and a four hour wait there, plenty of time," Artemus said. "No need to act as though we were venturing into the heart of the wilderness." His eyes glittered phlogiston-blue in what she'd learned to call his pranksome mood. "I'll bet you that he says three things to offend you before the soup arrives. What do you think, my dear Hasidic?"

She sighed. "All in a day's work," she retorted. She retreated into the compartment. At least there was time to change before dinner.

She wore sea-green to the meal, a silk-cotton blend that maintained its shape better than most garments when traveling. When she saw Belinda McCormick's pale brown silk taffeta, trimmed with Bruges, she wished she hadn't bothered, particularly when the professor's eyes flicked over her, assessing the color against the dark hue to her skin, pronounced after a month in Baltimore's sun.

Swarthy little girl, but sometimes those burn the hottest, he thought with a mental picture that kindled fire in her cheeks.

The table's center held a wire and ivory basket for a spray of fresh flowers and the condiments: cut glass containers of red and yellow and green sauce, tiny shakers of salt and pepper. She fixed her eyes on that. To her right, Belinda was a welcoming, quiet void. She found herself leaning and glanced over to find the girl looking at her with steady, inquisitive... invitation or naïveté? So hard to know, sometimes.

The other passengers spoke and chattered as they ate turtle consommé, a special Coast-to-Coast salad, and chicken-fried steak. Glasses of sherry were served round, though no one at their table took any. The Professor spoke primarily to his daughter, checking to make sure she knew the details of his trip, and what days and when he would be where. Artemus maintained his usual polite detachment.

Elpseth did the same. When a fat man lurched up from his table, at first she didn't react, lulled by the train's motion into a half-doze that barely noticed the warmth of his anger. Artemus, though, stood with immediate grace, interposing himself between the newcomer and McCormick.

"Necromancer!" the fat man spat at the Professor, who looked up but continued to chew his steak, placid-jowled and incurious as a cow. "Our President is not content to have sent the dead into the field against their own brethren, but now you assist Abraham the Unholy by raising the dead to bind them into machines." He pushed at Artemus, who budged not an inch. "Whose soul is bound into you, demon-machine?"

"No one's but my own, I assure you," Artemus replied.

Someone at one of the watching tables laughed and the angry man blushed, taking a step back. The steward appeared, taking his elbow to guide him out. The situation stopped ticking with menace as Artemus returned to his seat. The windows rattled in their frames, coffee cups clinked in after-dinner saucers, and they sped on along the prairie.

Elspeth removed herself at one point, vanishing to the johnny-car and returning with cheeks flushed.

Artemus leaned over as she sipped coffee to murmur, "What happened?"

She leaned back into her chair, trying to look official as she whispered into Artemus's aluminum-cast ear. "A woman wanted know what you were like in bed, offered me money for you."

"And?"

"And!? Should I pimp you out in order to make a little extra income along the way?"

He shrugged. "It's all data."

"You don't even know what to do, let alone have the equipment to do it!"

He quirked an eyebrow. "I am given from certain 'blue' materials that digital and lingual stimulation is sufficient. It's not as though the act would be about my own pleasure after all, other than the frisson of new experience. Still, I am told it is a valid way to persuade a witness or ally."

His tone remained impersonal but his eyes flickered an amused blue. She jerked away from him and turned her attention to Belinda.

"What do you hope to do in Seattle?" she asked.

The girl toyed with the food on her plate. Elspeth thought she'd eaten a few bites at most, perhaps even less. "I will continue to act as my father's assistant, of course," she said hesitantly.

"Of course you will," her father interrupted. His own plate shone; he'd used a roll to scrub the last of the gravy from the cold white china. He stared at Elspeth.

She doesn't keep kosher, his undermind said. *I wonder what else she is...unconventional in.*

After dinner, Elspeth lingered, sniffing hungrily at the draughts of cigar smoke that wafted her way.

"Think it's safe enough?" she overheard at her elbow. She craned her ears to listen.

"There was a werewolf attack last month, but since then they've put up silver," the other man said. The deck of cards riffled before he dealt them out. They whispered across the white linen tablecloth.

"And Snakes?"

"Snakes?" The other man spat out a laugh. Black stubble hazed his jaw. He caught Elspeth's eye and gave her a vulpine grin, sizing her up. Raising his voice, he said, "Snakes are what they use to scare passengers into behaving. Don't go anywhere by yourself, because you might get et.

That's just a way to keep pretty ladies from getting lured into shadows for kisses from nice men."

Elspeth refrained from joining the conversation. As a Pinkerton agent, she'd met plenty of supernatural creatures. She knew there were a few werewolves, or rather shapechangers, that lived in the wilderness in small families. She was less worried about Snakes, even though the semi-mythical creatures were blamed for nearly every disaster that claimed human lives.

In either case, this wasn't like England, overridden with all manner of creature, including werewolves, fairies and vampires.

The Professor sat puffing a cigar, working it with tight jaws. When it finally had burned to an inch's worth of stub, he caught Elspeth's eye and nodded at her to follow him as he rose. His mind revealed nothing other than the last of the tobacco's tang and a weary readiness for his bed.

She followed him through the several cars housing those unfortunate enough not to have the price of a sleeper, relegated to the hard wooden benches fastened to the walls. They smelled of sweat and cheese and garlic and stomach gas and she sensed herself perceived by minds sleep-clouded by motion and time spent staring forward waiting to arrive.

Outside the two compartments, the Professor paused.

Elspeth waited.

He looked everywhere but at her. "I want you to speak to my daughter."

"About?" His embarrassment burned in her stomach, incandescent as lava.

"She has always lived with me. Her mother died when she was three. Our domestic situation has made her isolated in a manner that has warped her."

"Such as?"

"She has become forward in unexpected ways," he said. His pink skin deepened in tone and he wiped at his brow with a crumpled silk handkerchief.

"The suffrage movement appeals to many young women who feels their own lives are circumscribed," Elspeth supplied. She'd seen this struggle before, including in her own family when she'd announced she planned to become a Pinkerton agent.

He shook his head. "There are many movements affecting the young nowadays. I was thinking more of the..." He hesitated, picking the words as carefully as making change out of a purse. "The movement that some people call Free Love."

Elspeth tried to school her face into a lack of expression, but a brow crept upward despite herself.

"She wishes to practice Free Love?" she said, very carefully. Where was Artemus? But her partner had said he wished to check the rest of the train. She wondered if he was looking for the woman who had offered Elspeth money for a couple of hours with him.

The Professor's hand flapped in the air like a trapped bird searching for windows of escape. "Tell her...tell her that things are not as simple as she would like to think when it comes to defying societal mores. For women there are consequences and they come when least expected or desired." He sighed.

There was something in his mind around all this that made Elspeth uneasy, but she nodded. They exchanged slight bows and retired into their compartments.

Artemus was back within a half hour, ready to set up watch. Elspeth did not question him as where he had been. Her partner's inability to sleep was a definite plus. It made simple sense to always have him be the one watching in the small hours of the night, when his human counterpart might fall prey to drowsiness.

So many pluses to partnering with him. Before him, she'd been assigned to a former Army colonel who had never quite gotten over the shock of working with a woman. For Artemus that had never been an issue, and chivalry was impersonal with him, a matter of his metallic brain and body outshining any human's, gender notwithstanding.

They'd spent a week last spring in the Pinkerton Academy and she'd had a chance to speak with other female agents, despite how few and far between they were. Chloe Louisiana was a mulatto and former slave who always partnered with another woman, a half-Shawnee who'd been raised in England and whose name was Persephone Godschild. They were all united in their hate of the only other female agent present, a southern sharpshooter, Belle Cheatham, whose disdain they had all dealt with in the past.

"You're lucky to have Artemus as your partner," Chloe had said. She glanced over at Persephone, who'd nodded. The three of them had been sitting in a classroom, comparing notes and waiting for an instructor in ballistics to arrive.

Elspeth hadn't understood. Back then she'd seen it as punishment, assigning the odd psychic to the only thing capable of dealing with her. She went back and forth on whether the assignment was punishment or praise. It felt like either with equal frequency.

She lay in bed. A thought occurred to her and she pulled herself out of the narrow bunk to press her face up to the cold glass of the tiny window. Outside the vast plains were silvered with moonlight and the train's long shadow raced beside them. Faint clouds seined the starry sky and somewhere a wolf howled.

Artemus shifted in the hallway. He'd heard her, she suspected, and wanted her to know her he was there if needed, without saying it outright.

Another one of the little gestures that seemed so unmechanical.

She returned to bed and lay there. The train said chuggadiggity-chuggadiggity-chuggadiggity and she dropped into sleep counting the syllables of that complex beat.

Someone scratching on her door woke her. She gathered her wrapper around her nightgown and slid the door open.

Belinda, in her own wrapper, embroidered with pale blue flowers and uncoiling ferns. No Artemus in the corridor, but the light in the other room suggested he was there with the Professor.

"Do you smoke?" Belinda said in a low whisper. Her eyes sparked as Elspeth nodded, and she held up two cigarettes in a conspiratorial way. "They're talking. We'll go indulge."

Outside, they sparked cigarettes alight with phosphorus matches in the doorway's shelter before moving to stand on the swaying platform as the dark world hurtled past.

Belinda exhaled. The smell of the tobacco flickered in Elspeth's nostrils. "You know what I want in Seattle?" she said.

Elspeth shook her head. It was so refreshing not to be able to pluck the answer out of the other's head, mystifying and giddying all at once, trying to figure out answers from clues as fragile and fleeting as cigarette smoke.

"I want to have a friend. Maybe several," Belinda said. She reached out with her free hand and scraped the back of her index finger along the soft flesh of Elspeth's inner arm.

Elspeth's heart jumped in her throat. In her mind, the Professor's voice said, ...*the movement that some call Free Love*. She didn't react to the touch and after a long moment, Belinda leaned back against the railing and took another puff from her cigarette.

Elspeth had opened her mouth to reply when something lunged out of the night, a snarl of claw and tooth and gray fur striking from the ground to land between them.

Belinda recoiled, colliding with the glass of the door even as Espeth's foot snapped out to catch the beast in the throat. She thanked her Pinkerton training, all the work she'd had to do to prove herself.

With a gabbled whine, the creature fell away. Elspeth grabbed Belinda and pulled her inside the car.

In its confines, the younger woman swayed, hand at her throat, eyes wide and fixed on Elspeth as her knees buckled.

Elspeth stooped to the floor as well, feeling the rocketing rails underneath through her shinbones, grappling Belinda to her.

Belinda's lips tasted of tobacco. Her heart hammered against Elspeth as Elspeth drew her into the compartment and the narrow, moon-washed bed.

She woke tangled in Belinda's arms to the sound of knocking on the door. Artemus' characteristic shave-and-a-haircut-two-bits.

"What is it?" she called.

"The Professor."

She gestured quiet at the wide-eyed Belinda as she pulled on her nightgown. "What about him?" she called through the doorway.

"His doorway is locked but he's not answering."

Artemus looked to her before fingering the lock. He was not supposed to pick mechanisms unless there was a human present.

She hoped that Belinda would have the sense to wait until they had entered the other cabin before making her way out of Elspeth's compartment.

The lock clicked open and Artemus's hand fell away. He flipped the handle open and swung it inward cautiously, as though afraid of waking the Professor.

Who was unwakeable, lying as he did in a pool of crimson and surprise, face agape.

As they stood there in the doorway, Belinda appeared behind them and gasped. "Papa!"

"I must ask you to stand back, Miss McCormick," Artemus said. "Elspeth, would you take her to a quiet place close by?"

"Like my cabin?" Elspeth said.

"That would do, certainly."

Elspeth escorted the wide-eyed, shocked Belinda back into the cabin and petted and soothed her for a few moments before returning to Artemus' side in the other compartment.

He stood frowning in the middle of the compartment. "I don't see it."

"See what?"

"The professor was carrying the formula for his work to the War Ministry."

She looked around the tiny space. "It's not here?"

"He has his case there, and another trunk full of presents. I believe for his host's children."

"What makes you think that?"

"I took the liberty of opening them. One is a puzzle, another a set of fables, and the third a board game, 'Snakes on a Train.'"

"So the killer must have taken the formula."

"Belinda is the most likely suspect."

Elspeth hoped Belinda would remember the brief story Elspeth had coached her in. "She went for coffee to the dining car but found it closed. He was alive when she left."

Artemus's expression ground into disapproval. He didn't like activating that portion of his face's mechanism, she knew, preferring to keep it a bland and unthreatening smile.

"I don't think it was her," she said firmly, and left it at that, hurrying on to say, "I think it'll be someone who gets off at the next stop."

"When is that?"

"For a major stop, one that is more than fuel? A day or so."

Summoned, two wide-eyed porters helped drag the body back several cars, wrapped in a blanket and supported as though it were an under-the-weather passenger, back to the refrigerator car.

After that, the Pinkerton agents canvassed the train to find the individuals planning on getting out at Kansas City. A young married couple, the Emersons, planning on joining Mrs. Emerson's brother's homestead nearby; a school-teacher headed into the Territory; two traveling sales-men, one in patent sun hats and soaps, and the other in tin-ware; two former soldiers headed to get jobs as cattle drovers; and a veterinarian who had just purchased a practice in Kansas City in the mail.

Neither Artemus nor Elspeth could extract any reason why any of these individuals would have reason to kill the Professor.

Artemus' expression was still disapproving. "The daughter..."

"It's not her," Elspeth said. "I think it's a wolf. We saw one when we were out there. One could jump onto a platform and come along a corridor."

"And have hands to open the door?"

"Were-wolves," she pointed out. "Shape-changers. Skilled ones can manage half-way forms."

"If there were such a creature then it is long gone," Artemus said.

"Let's question everyone," Elspeth said. "The man who called him a necromancer, for example."

That man turned out to be a Portland bound minister, Alexander Knolle. Roused from his own sleeping car and questioned as to how he knew what McCormick had been doing, he pointed out that it had not been much of a secret, since McCormick had spoken in several lyceums in the Baltimore and DC area in the week previous to boarding the train.

"He bragged on it," the fat man said sweating but adamant, gaze trembling between the two. "On how his formula help suit machinery and morbid flesh to each other. Morbid flesh, that's what he called it. Dead things. I fought in the war last year. I know what comes of that." He shuddered and retched.

The next night, Artemus spent on the platform watching for wolves.

Around two in the morning, Elspeth went out with him. The stars stretched overhead, brilliant as diamonds, lights that seemed close enough to reach up and pluck one.

"Is Belinda settled?" Artemus said over the rush of the wind and the rattle of the train.

"For now," Elspeth said. She titled her face away from him, knowing he'd be able to read any rush of heat to her cheeks. She said, over her shoulder, "When we were first assigned together, I didn't like it. Now I wouldn't have any other partner."

She wasn't sure whether or not he was aware of Belinda's scent clinging to her, of the phantom pressure of hands that clenched at her skin. Perhaps he'd think her blushes the result of her verbal confession. Either way, she wanted him to be reassured. "There's no one else I'd rather have." Silence stretched between them and she said, struck by it, "Can you say the same?"

"I am used to you," he said, but she thought some other emotion glinted far below the living light of his eyes.

Someone knocked on the partition. Belinda, pressed up against the glass.

"Someone's in with papa's things," she said. "I heard them knocking about."

They crowded in, Artemus first. The heavy musk of wolf musk hung in the air. Where they had searched through the Professor's things but kept them in order, someone else had executed no such caution, but rather flung drawers open, tumbled cases on the floor, and dumped belongings out onto the floor. The puzzle pieces lay underfoot mixed with a scattering of tea bags and the delicate bones of some bird's wing, mingled with some reptile's coiled spine.

"Looking for something." Artemus picked up a copy of a book and laid it on the bedspread.

"But what?" Elspeth said.

"The formula still."

"So it's whoever killed him but they still don't have the formula." Elspeth looked around the compartment. "Either because it's here hidden among his belongings, or because he's hidden it elsewhere on the train."

"Or because he never had it," Artemus pointed out.

Disappointment clenched at Elspeth's gut. "What makes you think that?"

"It seems as possible as anything else," Artemus said. He looked around at the mess. "Someone believes it's here, at any rate."

"If it's a werewolf, they'll surely try one last time before we hit the next town," Elspeth said. "How is he or she managing to keep up with the train?"

"They are supernatural creatures, endowed with uncanny amounts of speed and endurance," Artemus said. He didn't add that one of his appeals for the Pinkerton Agency was his ability to match those uncanny abilities.

They waited in the darkness. Artemus was braced in the cupboard space; Elspeth crouched near the door. Belinda was bundled in Elspeth's bed again with orders to bar the door and not come out for love or money. After those instructions had been given, the two Pinkertons had taken up position. They didn't speak.

The hours jolted by, the train slowing and speeding up. If she were the wolves, she'd wait for one of the curves where the train would be forced to deaccelerate, she thought. Even as it occurred to her, the axles squealed as they leaned left.

She tilted her head, listening, but also extending her other sense outward, searching for thoughts. There. *? where ?* was not the thought of any passenger but the frustration of someone looking for a specific thing, returning to search again. *river/camphor/dust* flared in her senses and said they were familiar, long familiar. She heard a sound she couldn't decipher, lost between the outer and the inner perceptions.

"They're trying to get into your room," Artemus said, moving to the door.

She followed after him in the darkness, wishing they'd told Belinda to wait elsewhere.

Sparks flared, a shot rang out.

Artemus shouted.

She struck a light in the silence to see him holding a lean and ragged wolf by the paw/wrist. Green eyes glinted, considering her. The toothy jaws opened and croaked out, "Hnake. Here. Kill Hnake."

She looked at Artemus, but his gaze confirmed her own senses. Sincerity.

They backed into the other tiny bedroom, debris and puzzle pieces crunching underfoot.

"You're looking for a Snake," Artemus said. "You sensed it, presumably."

The heavy muscle dipped in a nod. This close, Elspeth found that every instinct of her body screamed to get away. The green eyes blinked in amusement, considering her.

"It's Belinda," Artemus said.

"This again?" Elspeth said. "I know you don't like her."

"That has nothing to do with anything. She's the Snake. She's taken the actual daughter and disposed of her along the way. As a master illusionist, she's able to cloud your mind and make you think she's just a null."

Elspeth ran through matters in her head. The sheer weighty reluctance of doing so convinced her that Artemus was right. Something was very wrong with Belinda.

"Something more," Artemus said. He knelt and picked up a handful of puzzle pieces. "Look at the backs."

She turned over the carved wood with dawning realization. "Pencil marks on the back. It's his formula."

Artemus' blue eyes shuttered. "If the knowledge goes to the War Ministry, they will make machines from fallen soliders. So will anyone else who learns it." He methodically plucked puzzle pieces from the floor. "They are very flammable, these pieces."

This was why they assigned a human to the mechanical, to think out questions of judgment and justice. In theory. But it seemed he no longer needed her.

She took the pieces from his hands and shoved them in the waistband of her shirt. "If we just throw them out, there's still a chance someone could find and reassemble them."

He nodded. "The engine is three cars up."

But when she reached the engine, Belinda was there.

"Ahhhh," the young woman breathed out regretfully as she saw Elspeth's face. She spread her hands in a helpless gesture. "I take it the jig, as we say, is up?"

Elspeth took a few steps forward, looking at the door to the boiler, small and square and securely shut.

Before she could move again, Belinda's form blurred and interposed itself. Elspeth felt the hard muscles against her own.

"Would you like?" the voice buzzed, half out loud, half in mind. *Like to see what I really look like?*

She breathed out assent and the golden curls shimmered, gave way to a hood of shimmering scales, purple and pine and scarlet, and eyes that stared at her tenderly. She was enfolded in coils, and Belinda's mouth hovered over the vein that pulsed in her neck.

I will not touch your blood, the voice said in her head, *not for all the world, beloved, but oh, if I did, it would be right here* — the teeth dipped and grazed the skin in a circle of freezing pleasure that ran from that point down to her very core, where it warmed and made her loins heavy with desire — right here and the lips caressed the skin as though licking some flavor from them.

Even as that pleasure burned, Elspeth grappled the door open and threw the puzzle pieces in to flare up in a cascade of sparks. Even so, the arms held onto her waist, the warm breath caressed her shoulder. *It is a bad thing for anyone to hold, and there will be other power, given time,* the internal voice hissed, and suddenly nipped, not breaking the skin but making her gasp aloud with the intensity of the pleasure.

The orgasm shook her, drove her off her feet, and the arms released her to let her slide against the wall as the Snake backed away, green eyes amused and regretful.

We will meet again, you and I.

The door opened and the figure was gone, fallen out into the dark night.

"It is," Artemus said, "something that we can explain to the War Ministry. The professor died telling no one the formula. It died with him."

"You don't want to say that the emissary of a group of magical shape shifters killed him for it"? Elspeth asked.

Artemus shuddered. "We would face questioning for weeks." The amusement faded. "We'll have to find the group ourselves."

"If they don't find us first," she said. She heard the voice again, *beloved*, and then *there will be other power, given time.*

She looked to Artemus.

We will meet again, you and I.

And what will happen then?

Afternotes:

This story started, as you may have guessed, with the title. I had previously written "Her Windowed Eyes, Her Chambered Heart," and wanted to return to Artemus and Elspeth. Sharp readers will notice contradictions in the love story between the two; that is by design and will be explained in a forthcoming story.

Rappaccini's Crow

DOCTOR RAPPACCINI HAS A pet crow named Jonah. He says he raised it from a chick, but I have trouble imagining Doctor Rappaccini patiently nursing anything, tucking a blanket around it to keep it warm or feeding it mealworms and apple shards. If he has such a faculty for tenderness, he doesn't exhibit it towards any of the patients here.

Today he made an appearance to supervise Mr. Abernathy's removal from his wheelchair.

Someone should have realized Abernathy was never moving from it, but the orderlies probably welcomed not having to lift him back and forth. Bedsores must have formed while he sat there. Over the weeks, they split and healed, split and healed, finally fusing him to the wicker.

The orderlies left him there, looking out over the garden's distant purple leaves. Never showing any sign of pain, till his flesh grew into the chair. Today at 2:45 PM, he screamed while they cut it away, and Doctor

Rappaccini and his crow watched, unspeaking. When they were done, he leaned forward to listen to Mr. Abernathy's heart with his stethoscope. By then Abernathy had lapsed into silence, but I wondered that Rappaccini could hear the beat of the man's heart over the painful wheeze of his lungs.

The Doctor wears a pad on his shoulder for the crow to shit on. It misses most of the time, and gray and white clots the black coat's backside.

It's hit or miss whether Abernathy will survive. I don't know that he cares either way.

Before this, all he did was stare out his window, day and night, past purple and green leaves towards the east, towards the mountains the white men call the Cascades.

Over the mountains, they tell me, the sun shines all the time.

Thunder last night. Not natural thunder, but echoes from the unending battle being waged far out among the San Juans. The great phlogiston-fueled battle rafts crash against each other day and night, pushing their claim to territory back and forth. We're close enough to those battle lines that many people have fled south to Oregon. Others have stuck it out, saying that the lines will shift again, in a different direction.

I have stayed. Where else would I go?

I wheel the Colonel out into the watery sunlight. He can walk, but he prefers the dignity of the chair, in spite of its awkwardness, to having to struggle for every step.

Two days ago, when he surrendered his artificial leg to me after a visit from his niece, the Colonel said, "I knew every man of the three who owned this before me."

He slapped the cloudy brass surface of the calf. "And some fella will get it after me. Maybe someone I know, maybe someone I don't. Do you think ghosts linger around the objects they leave behind? If so, I'd be surprised if there weren't three ghosts riding this one."

I didn't answer, and he didn't expect me to. He knows my vocal cords were seared away in the same war that stole his leg. The same war that's furnished most of the inhabitants of this asylum. Broken soldiers, minds and bodies ground-up by its terrible machines.

Used to be an injury was enough to get you out. Now if they can, they turn you into a clank, half human, half machine, and send you back to the endless task of pushing the lines back and forth. Nowadays we receive only the men who cannot be repaired, and here they sit or lie in their beds, waiting to die a slower death than the war would have given them, tended by orderlies like me, other broken men and women who can function enough to pretend to work.

People forget. Even though I can't speak, I can still hear. Or maybe they don't forget that. Maybe they just figure I'll never be able to tell anyone.

True enough. I don't have many who understand hand signs here in the asylum. But I can write out messages, even if it takes me a long time to construct the letters, even if they waver and bobble in a way that got me beaten over and over by the nuns back in school. As though your relationship with God was reflected in the character of your handwriting.

I don't see Dr. Rappaccini that much. But that crow goes everywhere in the asylum. No one pays it much mind. It flaps along corridors and perches on the back of chairs, goes into patient rooms and pokes through their dressers. Mr. Whitfield told me it took his wife's wedding ring, which he'd had on the night table in a china saucer so he could look at it when he first woke up.

Maybe the crow took it. Or maybe another orderly slipped it in his pocket, thinking to himself that we're not paid that much, or at least not enough to be able to resist temptation. I don't know.

Either way, even if Mr. Whitfield lost it himself, he cried when he told me about it; ineffectual old man sobs. I patted his shoulder, feeling how thin and bony it was under the threadbare garment. Dr. Rappaccini says Mr. Whitfield is one of the lucky ones. His body wasn't harmed by the war. Instead he has war shock, pieces of his mind blown away instead of his flesh.

Is he truly one of the lucky ones? Sometimes I think that must be; having something broken in your head must be better than having something broken in your body, visible to anyone who looks at you.

Other times I'm not so sure.

I watched the crow this morning, thinking that if it had taken Mr. Whitfield's ring, it would have put it somewhere. That it would have some treasure trove of what it'd stolen, somewhere in the asylum, and that I'd be able to retrieve the ring from it.

Mr. Whitfield was so upset. His white hair stood up in startled tufts and his eyes oozed tears. It was as though all his soul was in that ring. He told me that it was the only thing that let him remember his wife.

So I watched the crow. It made its rounds like a doctor, room to room, checking on each patient. I hadn't noticed that before. Who would; who has time to watch a crow, here where we are overworked, where every idle hand is quickly put to labor?

It's odd how everyone seems to defer to it, almost as though it is Dr. Rappaccini himself. The only person who dares defy it is the cook, when she shoos it away from the beef roast being readied for the dinner.

She never speaks of her past, but it surfaced in her language, the spray of invective, filthy and informative, spat in the crow's direction.

She flung a saucepan at the crow as well. The crash as it hit the wall cupboard made everyone in the kitchen jump. Everyone looked around, afraid that Doctor Rappaccini might have seen .

He wasn't there, but the crow was indignant enough for both of them. She was lucky it couldn't talk, couldn't tell the doctor what she had done to his beloved pet. It hopped away on the counter, then flapped up to the high shelf held up with iron corbels and perched there, clacking its beak and cawing at her as though about to explode with indignation.

She went over to the window above the sink and opened it, stepped back, and gestured at it. As though it understood her, the crow flapped and flew out, still berating her with squawks and quonks.

By evening though, it seemed to have forgiven her. Or maybe it was taunting her, I don't know which. Either way, it hopped on her shoulder as she was trying to ladle out dinner to the shuffling rows of patients. She couldn't push it off, since the doctor was standing there watching.

But it couldn't resist payback. She showed me later the blood on her arm where its claws had dug in, a cluster of discolored oozing marks. If I could have, I would've told her to wash it. I tried to mime that out. Demons live where there is dirt, and who knows what kind of demons a crow harbors? Instead she wrapped it back up, winding the bandage around her arm, hiding the damage.

Last night I dreamed I was the crow.

Crows aren't male and female the way we are. Or at least it's a matter of indifference to humans, and something that presumably only matters to other crows. I flew among men AND women and all of them looked at me and knew that I wasn't like them, but that was all right, because I was a crow.

Other parts of being a crow were less appealing. I flapped my wings and made a gravelly sound in my throat as I plucked an eyeball from a corpse. I popped it in my beak like a grape squeezed between thumb and forefinger, full of juice, to the point where it burst, spattering liquid over my wings.

I woke with a coppery taste in my mouth.

Over breakfast, I watched outside where Jonah sat on the fence post, calling to the other crows. None of them came down to sit with him, no matter how much he cooed or wheedled. Several times he flapped up to try and land beside them. Each time they pecked at him until he flew away.

No one else seemed to notice except the Colonel. He caught my eye and said, "Probably doesn't smell right to them. Doesn't smell the way a proper crow should."

So Jonah pays some price for his life here. It must seem worthwhile to him, or he wouldn't stay.

Perhaps that's why his temper is so nasty; why he cannot stand to be thwarted.

I wonder what the other crows must think of Jonah. A crow that's allowed itself to be tamed in order to make its life more comfortable. Do they envy it, or think it's sold its soul?

If there was someone else like me, what would that reflection say about me?

Would he envy me?

Or think I've sold my soul?

Sometimes prejudice works to my advantage. I don't have to share a room with any of the other orderlies, because they are white and don't want to sleep with the dirty Indian.

That saves me trouble. I can unwind the bandages around my breasts and breathe.

I'm still a man. That's what I feel like.

But sometimes my body doesn't agree.

It's always been that way. I knew I was a man, even when everything else was telling me differently. It wasn't until I ran away from the orphanage, lied and enlisted in a war that was eating up soldiers faster than anyone could produce them, that I could live the way I wanted to.

It wasn't something I could have accomplished on my own. Here and there people have helped, looked the other way or let me slide by. When I was injured, of course the doctors knew. They could've caused a scandal. As it was, all they did was make sure I couldn't draw on my pay, because I'd accumulated it under false pretenses, or my pension, which fell into the same category.

But there is plenty of work for those no longer fit to be soldiers. My options, the options offered an Indian who could no longer speak, were certainly not those offered someone with paler skin or whose gender was unquestionable, but I did all right.

I could probably find better employment than an asylum for those broken by the war. But here, there are so few questions, so little time for looking at those around us, that it hopefully will always be safe for me, even though all of us are overworked and underpaid. I can find what comfort I can here, in a world where there is so little.

Cook died last night.

Sepsis, Doctor Rappaccini said. From some small injury she must have sustained in the kitchen and carelessly left untreated. He said the word "carelessly" as though her death was just a matter of her being too stupid to take care of herself.

He didn't say that she was a careful woman who kept things as clean as she could. He didn't say that she tried her best for the patients, to comfort them not with her body as she once had but by making the food less wretched. She was good at bargaining on the black market, and she never used those skills to enhance her own table, only to get suet or sugar or spices that might make them happy for a moment when they tasted a favorite dish.

The replacement that Dr. Rappaccini finds for her will not make anyone happy but him. He doesn't own the asylum outright but he might as well, having been appointed by the board of directors after he'd convinced them that he could make it turn a profit. That seems odd, to think that an asylum can be profitable, but at the heart of things it is a business.

And a business that the doctor knows well, in terms of how to cut corners. Before he came, patients wore their artificial limbs every day, a practice that Rappaccini says only leads to wear and breakage. Back then whenever someone died, their artificial limbs were buried with them. Now they're wiped down with a solution of Condy's Crystals and put away to be used again and again.

Food arrives from the War Office each week. Never enough. The cook used to send the off-duty orderlies out to forage for greens to supplement what there was. Some grumbled, but it was in our best interest to cooperate.

The first day I foraged, I was so pleased to bring her back several armloads of fiddleheads. I knew they were edible, although I had never seen ones before with such a faint purplish hue to them.

She made a face and picked one up to sniff it. She shook her head, setting it down, and said, "Boy, you took these from the Doctor's garden?"

I had been here only a few days and didn't know what she meant. My face showed it.

She said, "Come with me."

She led me to the garden where I'd found the ferns. Surrounded by cypress, it seemed half-abandoned at first. A fountain, its white marble confines crumbling, burbled and splashed in the center, wild iris flowering around it in shades of blue and purple. But when I looked closer, I realized many of the plants were caged in urns and other containers. The largest stood next to the fountain, a bush covered with purple flowers, brilliant as gems, so lovely they seemed to illuminate the garden when a cloud flickered over the sun.

"You don't come here, and neither do you bring me any food from it," the cook directed. She was thin and wiry. Freckles splotched her skin, the color of weak cocoa. "You stay away from it." She pointed at the flowering plant. "See that? Another month and it'll fruit. Don't go eating those or you'll regret it. This is the doctor's personal garden."

I can glimpse that garden now as we line up around the grave, in the cemetery that adjoins our grounds. An unobtrusive white stone, skull-sized, rolls in the grass to mark each dead patient. Name and dates applied with black paint that wears away quickly, leaving a shadow like a day's worth of stubble on the cold stone.

The priest says, "Let us pray."

I close my eyes to hear the breathing of the men around me, the shuffle of their feet and crutches, the creak of wheelchairs.

"Requiem Aeternam dona eis, Domine, et lux perpetua luceat eis…"

I always associate the sound of Latin with furious whispers, with sharp pinches. With eyes like freshly broken blue/black/brown glass beads, pressing down from an adult's height over my vantage point as a child.

The nuns were unhappy with their assignment to an institution devoted to making Navajo children assimilate into white culture, and the children were the closest outlet for that frustration.

I was six when they came for me and my two brothers. They split us up and sent us to different schools. That was the rule, break up the families. They didn't want Indian children banding together, didn't want them telling each other memories of home, reminding each other of what they had left behind.

We could not call ourselves The People any longer. They wouldn't let us speak our own language. If we spoke in Navajo, they beat us; forced us to find the English words to say what we wanted. Not that they would have given us anything we wanted.

In the mornings, we ate burned bread and cold oatmeal and listened to Sister Perpetua barking out the day's reading from the Old Testament. She looked like a china doll from a Christmas tree, but she didn't talk like one. She never seemed to pick the Bible's kinder parts, only the pieces calculated to frighten us. The story of the prophet Elijah telling bears to eat the wicked children who'd mocked his bald head was her favorite.

We heard the Bible at breakfast, and at the noon snack, and at dinner. We swam in stories from the Bible, all of them telling us how wrong we were. They told us we could never be like whites; they told us we had to be like whites. On Sundays, they prayed over us from dawn to dusk. I never understood how they could despise us so yet devote their lives to teaching us.

So few of them seemed happy. So many of them seemed ready to lash out at us, swift as a scorpion, angry in a way that confused and bewildered me.

But for every few dozen scorpions, there was someone whose presence outweighed the rest. Like Father McNeill.

He was tall, so tall. I'd never seen a man stretch that high before. You would've thought it would have made him frightening. But he had a way of leaning down to listen, blue eyes intent, that made him comforting.

He was head of the school when I came there. He stood at the entrance as they marched us in, two dozen Navajo children from Monument Valley and the Bears Ears and Moenkopi. Unhappy and frightened, and not knowing what sort of place we had come to.

His smile made us feel better, at least some of us. Others had learned already that when whites smile, sometimes they don't mean it.

Father McNeill meant it. He talked to each of us. He told me that Jesus was my friend, a friend I could always rely on. A friend who would comfort me.

I liked that. I liked the idea of a friend in those lonesome times. And some of the pictures of Jesus didn't make him look like a white man. I couldn't imagine him a Navajo like me, but I could imagine him a cousin from very far away. I liked the Jesus that Father McNeill talked about, a kind and loving and honorable man. A man someone could try to emulate.

In years that followed, I got a chance to compare stories with other children who'd been shipped off to places that didn't have anyone like Father McNeill. It was only then that I realized how lucky we'd been.

He kept things sane for us. It could have been much, much worse.

Much, much worse came later, after he died, and the school became like all the rest.

When I was sixteen and they finally let me leave, I tried to go home. I went back to Bears Ears, three days of hitching and walking. When I got there, my family was gone. No one remembered them. One fellow thought they'd moved over to Calamity Springs, so I went there too, but the trail was even colder there.

I had no money, no family, no home. So I signed up to serve in the War.

❧

Once you've noticed something, you notice it always. I watched Jonah the Crow. I couldn't help but notice him now.

At least I thought the crow was a him. Something about the way it cocked its head whenever Rappaccini spoke to it made me think that the two of them must share a gender.

The bird made his rounds every day like clockwork, checking to see what was happening, as though worried that he would come across a situation Rappaccini would not approve of. I could imagine the bird reporting to him, squawking out stories of inefficiencies and broken rules; informing on us all.

People ignored the crow, the same way that they ignored me. If you can't talk, you become just part of the background.

It's more comfortable being part of the background, being unnoticed and unquestioned. Neither the crow nor I were the first to discover that. But it's something that had served me well, during my time in the war.

We are not supposed to talk to the Colonel about the war. Dr. Rappacini is convinced too much emotion will cause apoplexy, that his heart will collapse under the strain. He doses the Colonel with opium, which gives him strange dreams.

Yesterday the Colonel told me his leg talks to him when he's asleep. He said, eyeing me, "Is that the strangest thing you've ever heard?"

I shrugged and shook my head.

"There's plenty of odd things in war, my boy," he said. He saw me raise an eyebrow at him and shrugged himself, although he flushed. "Yes, I know you're not my boy. You're just an Indian. But you're a man, like I am. You had a father. I had a son."

I didn't say anything, of course. More importantly I didn't gesture to contradict him.

He continued, hurriedly, as though to not give me time to reply, "Anyhow, the war is about phlogiston. You know what that is, how it powers the great engines that drive the city's heart. Not as much now, since almost all of that is devoted to the war effort." He spoke with conviction now, animated by his own words. "That's the contradiction at the heart of the war, see! Fighting over a precious resource, and using all of that resource in the fight. They keep saying that once the war is over, humanity will advance, once it's got all that phlogiston to devote to its own noble needs. But that will never happen. They're too evenly matched. And too many people are making money from supplying the machines to fight the wars. It won't stop." He paused and lowered his voice, forcing himself calm. "It won't stop till all of us are dead."

If I'd been able to speak, I would have. But all I could do was pat his shoulder and hope he understood.

II.

It's quiet here when no one is screaming. That's the biggest difference between here and the war: the noise.

There, it's everywhere — the cannons' boom, the machines' roar, the furnaces' blast, rockets shrieking, voices screaming. When I think of the war, that's what echoes through my head, pushing out the smell of iron and electricity and blood and salt water.

I lied about so many things when I enlisted. They didn't question any of it. They knew that most of the boys signing their names to enlistment papers were too young for it to be legal. But a war requires bodies, and it is not choosy about what kind they are.

I was assigned as a driver to a captain. Even now, when times are so desperate that they are taking thirteen year-olds, they don't allow the People to be soldiers. We were support staff only. I couldn't fight, but I could fly the little ornithopter that took him from ship to raft, from one battle to another.

The first time I saw the captain, I thought he was ugly. His face looked as though someone had thrown it together from lumps of clay. But his eyes were dark and long-lashed, like a woman's, almost too pretty. He was tall but stooped, as though to hide just how tall he was. His hair was so black it had a blue sheen underneath, like sunlight on a crow's wing.

He didn't like me anymore than I liked him. He didn't think he needed a driver; saw it as a way for the high command to restrict what he did. But after a while, he came to realize that I was useful and discreet.

He didn't start talking to me, really, until after a trip in which the side got blown off the ornithopter. I'd kept flying, pulling forward as shells clattered and boomed beside us.

It was early morning, and the sun was rising, revealing us. I knew I had to get us to safety, and I steered up, trying to gain the shelter of the clouds even as a shell exploded a few feet to my left, throwing smoke and fragments across the windshield, darkening the interior before the slipstream swept it away, a metal shard rasping across the glass.

The captain knew better than try to direct me, for which I was grateful. So many people think the best response to a crisis is to inject themselves into it. Instead he kept quiet and let me fly. Some corner of my mind, not occupied like the rest of it with the simple matter of survival, was warmed by that trust.

I earned it. We were shaken but unscathed by the time we landed. The only mark of the journey was the arc the shard had cut into the windshield, a curve that glinted in the full morning sunlight.

I was so glad to be alive.

The captain said, clapping me on the shoulder, "That was fine flying." He mistook my flinch at his touch and apologized.

I just nodded. Let him think that I didn't like other people touching me. That was easier than the truth.

I don't know when I realized he wasn't ugly anymore. It would've been some time after it was already too late. I had already fallen into love.

I didn't do anything with it. I'd never felt like that before. So I kept it like a hand-warmer in my pocket. Every once in a while I stole a glance at him and put the picture away in my mind, and used it to warm my heart, in the nights when I could hear the shells and everything was cold and lonely and too, too close to death.

I thought so many times about revealing myself to him. Telling him who I was.

But what did I expect would happen? Every time I played it out in my head, it never went the way I would've wanted it to. That dream required too much taking-in at the seams. It didn't fit what would happen. It was impossible to make it fit what would happen.

What does it say, when your deepest yearnings are so unrealistic you can't make them work even in your imagination? Does that say something about imagination's limitations, or, as it seems more likely to me, does it say something about that dream?

It's not that he didn't like women. He did, I knew that for sure. But I didn't want to come to him as a woman. That's not how I wanted him to love me. I wanted him to love me in the way that two men love each other.

Was that unreasonable?

It didn't seem that way at the time.

III.

The crow can tell one person from another. He knows who will flap at him and who will not notice his presence. And it uses that information.

I saw it hop onto Mr. Paper's shoulder. It had realized that he would just keep staring forward at the horizon, as he has done for three years now. The crow leaned over and grabbed a tuft of white hair in its beak and pulled, savage and fast.

Mr. Paper still didn't react, but I did. I ran forward and flapped my hands at the crow until it flew away, the hair still dangling from its beak and blood dripping down to Mr. Paper's back.

That was when I decided to kill it.

I couldn't do it openly. Dr. Rappaccini would have wreaked revenge on anyone who killed his pet. I had to think the murder through as carefully as though I were plotting to kill a human. Had to do it surreptitiously, in a way that couldn't be traced.

I thought about violent ways to do it. Catch it in a window and smash it, or find some cat or dog to kill it. But that seemed unworkable.

Here in the hospital it's easy enough to find poison, if you need it.

I took the potassium permanganate crystals from the Condy's Crystals jar, purple as sunset hills. If I could get the crow to ingest them, it would surely die.

I spent today watching to see what it ate, what delicacies tempted him.

Cheese. He liked cheese. So I took a lump of greasy orange cheddar from the icebox where it was stored for the doctor's snack and put the crystals inside. I rolled it into a lump, warming it against my flesh so it would be malleable, a yellow sticky lump with death at its center. I set it out in a room where I knew the crow would come, on a china plate on Mr. Paper's bedside table, because I knew he wouldn't take it before the crow.

It was a terrible mistake.

I underestimated the crow, silly though that sounds.

At first I thought my plan would work. But when has anything in life ever gone the way I thought it would? The crow hopped forward on the table, head tilted to see the cheese, turning its beak to see around it and to look with first one eye and then the other, as though weighing it.

I held my breath.

It looked at me.

It saw me. It looked at me watching it, and it realized what was going on, stabbed its beak into the cheese, not to pick it up but to reveal what lay at the core. And then, watching me all the while, it ate every bit of cheese from around the crystals but left them lying there.

It stared at me. I stared back. It was seeing me, not just an anonymous human. Me and me alone.

Who would have known that a bird could become your enemy? It seems comical. But those blank, black eyes, glittering at me, were anything but funny. It turned its head again, examining me first with one eye then the other.

I knew it would remember me. I knew it knew what I had meant to do.

But what could it do, really? It was just a bird. Not capable of speech. Or at least of communicating what it knew to anyone.

Still, it scared me.

When I was twelve, Sister Madonna came to the school. She came all the way from Italy, across the ocean, very far away. She was dark-skinned like an Indian, although her face was the wrong shape. But she looked, if you squinted, a lot like the women at home.

She was kind, too. Like Father McNeill, she was someone who managed to make all the others seem as though they didn't matter so much. When she patted you on the shoulder, you could feel the touch much later like a ghost; could lie in bed and summon up the way that the pressure had felt,(Linked Comment) reassuring. Full of love.

I had learned by then to hide myself away. My soul was like a turtle that had stuck its head out too many times, until all it wanted to do was stay inside the shell. But even turtles like the sunshine, like to crawl up on logs and feel the fierce heat beat down upon the plates of their hard shell. Sister Madonna was like that sun, that kind and welcoming heat.

That was why I confided in her.

I might not have been able to write much, might have had to struggle with that to the point where the nuns shrilled at me for the way my letters straggled, but it didn't mean that I was stupid.

I was clever in other ways. I could add up numbers at a glance or sort formulas fuzzed with x's and y's and z's into coherency as easily as combing out a greasy hank of wool. I was quick at counting, good at estimating. That's why I was tapped to help her when she took inventory in the storeroom, counting the papers and pencils and notebooks and all the other school supplies that they sent from the East in order to make us civilized.

It was a spring day. She asked me several times if I would rather be outside, but I was content to sit there listening to her chatter in her thick accented voice. She had a habit of humming to herself, and you'd hear scraps of hymns and sometimes whatever had been sung in chapel that Sunday.

I didn't bring it up. She asked me first. She said, tilting her head to one side to examine me, "What's troubling you, Vivian?"

When I came to the school, I tried to keep my old name, but this was the one they gave me, Vivian. By then it felt as natural to me as the other one. Which is to say, it was a woman's name and therefore not something that I wanted. But then I learned that it could be a man's name too.

I said to her, "Did you ever hear of women changing into men?"

She said, "Why would they ever want to do that?" And she laughed, but not in an unkind way.

I said to her, "I don't want to be a girl, Sister Madonna. If I pray to God hard enough, will he make me a boy?"

She took a breath and put the box down that she'd been counting through. She looked at me directly. She said, "God has decided what you are."

I said, "Then didn't God make it so that I would want to be a boy?"

She said, "Maybe it's a test from God. Is that what it feels like, a test?"

I shook my head.

She didn't say anything.

I said, "I don't feel like this body is mine."

I was afraid she would turn away, that she would tell me I was a bad thing, that all of these thoughts had been sent from the devil who, apparently, was the origin of many bad things, including the Navajo language and all the old ways.

But she didn't.

Instead she said, "Sometimes people are not suited to what the world wants of us. To know yourself in the right place is a comfort, and there is so little comfort in the world. Traditionally that's why many men and women have entered the church. Do you think that's where your calling is?"

I shook my head immediately. I didn't mean her any disrespect, but I had been there long enough to know that the church and I were not suited to each other.

"Well," she said, "sometimes what the world wants of us and what God wants of us are not the same. If you ask Jesus, he will tell you what to do. You can always turn to him. You know that, don't you?"

I did. Most of us resisted what we were told, but I had picked out bits to keep. Jesus was love, Father McNeil and Sister Madonna insisted. I liked that. I liked the idea of someone made from love, incapable of feeling hate.

Sister Madonna was the one who taught me how to bind my breasts when they emerged, so I could pass for a man when I wanted. She taught me that men and women move differently, not because their bodies are so different but because the world looks at them in such a different way.

The first day I walked out in boy's clothes, I couldn't believe that anybody didn't see I was a girl; that God didn't look down and make me burst into flame. But it felt so natural, like I had put on shoes that had been made just for me.

At least a few of the military recruiters knew I wasn't a boy. But I wasn't the only woman enlisting. They would have looked the other way even if we had been some new species. That's how desperate they were for bodies to wage their war. It didn't matter whether those bodies had a particular set of organs or not. They died the same either way.

The crow kept watching me. Wherever I went, I could look up and see its eyes upon me. Was it that it had realized I posed some danger to it, that it didn't want to let me sneak up on it again?

It wasn't that though. I was its next prey.

I didn't realize that until I saw it out in the moon garden. It hopped up on the edge of the center urn and reached out, not with its beak, but with a foot. It took a purple berry in its talons and squeezed until juice oozed out over its claws. It repeated the act with its other foot.

I remembered the marks on the cook's arm, the festering wounds. So small to have killed her. So very small that no one realized it was no accident.

That thought came with another one. I was as crazy as any patient ever shipped back from the lines, whose mind had been blasted to bits by the sound of the guns, by the deaths, by the senselessness of it all. Now I was imagining things, thinking that a bird was capable of thought, of premeditation. Of plotting someone's death.

I went outside for a walk, to try to clear my head, but all I could do was look at the birds and wonder. Maybe they were all part of it together. Maybe they all had some plot at their heart, of revenge… But revenge for what? For schoolboys taking eggs from their nests? For women wearing feather plumes on their hats? It seemed so trivial.

I remembered the crows watching Jonah, staring down at him from the drooping lines of a cedar tree's branches. No, there was no mass conspiracy among the birds. I did not need to flinch whenever I saw a sparrow. I only needed to concern myself with Jonah.

But how to go about that, I wasn't sure.

I woke, not knowing what had pulled me out of sleep. The war had left me, unlike so many, more capable of sleep than when I had entered;

the soldier's ability to grab a few quick winks whenever the opportunity presented itself.

For a moment, I thought I was back there. That I could lift my head from my cot and see the captain in the tent's vestibule going over papers and maps while I waited in case he needed me to fly him somewhere. Anywhere.

But in reality /But actually this was my room in the asylum, part of the converted slave quarters, a narrow and noisome space unadorned by any amenity. Other inhabitants of the ward pinned up postcards or silky scarves or drew on the boards in chalk, at any rate did something to make the space their own, to make it show some mirror of their personality.

I had no interest in anyone finding out more about me than they needed to. My walls were bare.

I had gone to sleep with the window open. Seattle stays cool until the beginning of July, when it hurtles into heat. I'd hoped for a cool wind to stir the stagnant, warm air. No breeze whispered, but there was something outlined in the window.

Jonah, perched on the sill. Watching me. I saw the glitter of his eyes. There was no reason to think some errant crow had come to investigate me. I had never seen a crow at night before. It could only be my enemy. Watching me sleep.

What plans might a bird hatch?

IV.

The Colonel died yesterday. Last night I dreamed of him, but he washed away and I was back in the dream.

It's the one that comes each night. Every time, the same. I see the gas cloud hanging there, roiling with red shadows. Try as I might to dodge it, its depths swallow me again. I try to hold my breath but cannot, eventually taking a breath that sears my lungs, burns away the tissues.

I've stood beside Rappaccini while he dissected a corpse. I know what ordinary vocal cords look like; where they are buried in the body. Rappaccini has pointed them out to me, beneath the epiglottis, above the trachea, talking all the while about how mine must differ, scarred by the harsh gas, as though it was my throat beneath his knife.

I remember flying through the cloud, thinking that if I moved fast enough we'd escape. I told the captain to throw the blanket over himself, to crouch down. That saved him. But the crimson gas seeped into the ornithopter, fingers prying into the window cracks, drifted up through the vents. I breathed it in, swallowed it despite how each gulp burned in my throat, keeping it from reaching him.

I was lucky. Another year and they might have made me into a clank. But back then, they were still dismissing people when they were injured, not holding onto them the way they do now.

The captain came to see me in the field hospital carrier, so close to the lines that the guns still thundered to punctuate his words. He cried, though not much, just a few tears as he held my hand and told me how sorry he was, how he'd put me in for a medal. Told me that he'd look for me after the discharge.

I thought about telling him then. But I couldn't speak; could only have tried to explain through pantomime and writing, knowing that the words would be inadequate. I couldn't tell him enough, couldn't say that I didn't want him to love me for the body that had been forced on me, I wanted him to love who I was, a man loving him.

That was important. But how could I convey that to him in my poor attempts at written language, that awkward scrawl that Sister Perpetua had burned my knuckles for?

I prayed that night for guidance, the way that Father McNeil and Sister Madonna had told me that I could always do. I turned to Jesus, my friend Jesus, to tell me what I should do, how I should act, and I laid all of that in his hands.

The next morning I felt refreshed and strengthened. Jesus would help me endure. I'd tell the captain, and he would be surprised at first but accepting, or perhaps he would tell me he'd suspected it all along.

Together, we would work it all out.

They wheeled me out into the morning, and I saw him walking towards me on the deck.

The guns thundered again.

Everything was noise and confusion and shouting and the smell of blood. My ears rang, and every sound came to me as though I were underwater.

The smoke cleared, drifted down as though unable to hold itself in the air any longer, and I saw him lying there.

His head was half gone, torn away by the shell. You/I could see his brains, the color of cold oatmeal, darkened by burns, lying in a pool of red. His eye was open and surprised, still long-lashed and pretty.

Still so pretty, even then.

That was God's message. That he hated me so much he would rather kill a good man than let him be sullied by my love.

God's writing was as ugly as mine. But it told me what I needed to know. That Father McNeil and Sister Madonna were wrong.

Jesus didn't love me. He wasn't my friend.

He was like all the rest of them.

V.

I could have gone back home after the war. But it wasn't my home anymore. The school hadn't made me white, but it made me no longer a Navajo, no longer understanding those ways or those stories. I had come to Seattle because it was so green back then, back before the factories had grimed all the trees.

I was helping clean Mr. Abernathy's old room, readying it for the next occupant. Doctor Rappaccini had made us try to clean the wheelchair up so it could be used again, but such a stench had permeated the wicker that even he was forced to admit it would never serve another patient. The stench even clung to the room's faded wallpaper, and I'd been directed to wipe that down with bleach-water.

I turned around and found the Doctor standing in the doorway. Jonas was perched on his shoulder. He said, "Mr. Zonnie, I'd like to talk with you."

That phrasing made me shiver. I'd never heard him call anyone Mister before, and it wasn't that there was respect edging the tone. Only menace.

He said, "There's been some things reported missing. Small thefts. A wedding ring, a medal."

I widened my eyes and looked puzzled.

"Some cheese intended for my meal," he continued, watching my face.

I kept it impassive, trying not to react. I don't know that I succeeded. The Doctor kept staring at me. I could smell the acrid, sour smell from the birdshit on his back. Jonah clacked his beak at me.

"You could be sent back to the war," the doctor said. Each time he paused between words, the crow clacked its beak again. Its head darted forward and I flinched.

The doctor noticed. "You're scared of a bird?"

I just kept still.

He said with scorn in his face, "What do you think a bird can do to you? Let's see."

He shrugged his shoulder. Jonah flew at me, all sharp beak and extended talons, raking at my face.

I made a noise — something rough and ragged and painful in my throat — and flung my arm up, trying to dislodge it. Warmth ran down my face and the beak plunged once, digging itself into the skin at the corner of my eye.

I rocked back, thinking he wanted my eye, that he wouldn't be satisfied till it was gone. I doubled over, shielding my head as the crow tore at me and Rappaccini watched.

Finally the Doctor said, "Enough."

The crow stopped stabbing at me. I heard the flap of its wings as it returned to his shoulder.

The Doctor's voice was cold. "Tomorrow's an inspection. Take the brass appliances and make sure they shine."

After the two of them were gone, I washed my face, thinking of the crow dipping its claws in the berries. I stole more crystals and dropped them in water, seeing the pink tinge spread across it before I used it to wash the wounds, ignoring its sting. The damage was bad, but my eye was unscathed, despite the torn skin beside it.

I tried not to think of the crow as I washed brass limbs with soapy water before drying them and taking up the brass polish, which smelled of ammonia and dust. I tried not to think that I had been asleep while that black thing hopped across the floor, perhaps perching on the end of the bed to look at me, to watch my eyeballs rolling beneath the paper-thin skin while he thought about plucking them out.

What was the crow? Because that's how I think of it, not by the name the doctor has given it. It seems unlikely that it is the name it would have chosen for itself.

Back with the nuns, they would have told me it was an instrument of the devil, summoned by sin, bent on taking souls down to hell, to drown in the lake of fire and brimstone. If not the devil himself, one of his imps.

Someone else might wonder if it was a human soul, born anew into the feeble body of a bird, frustrated by its lack of hands and speech, bent on destroying those born into superior bodies or else carrying out some ancient grudge incurred before it was ever hatched.

Or a skinwalker, a witch who takes on animal form?

Or maybe it was just a monster.

Just because the world held monsters didn't mean that God had made them.

When I was done, I staggered back to my room, hands aching. Something tapped on the window. I looked up to see the crow sitting there, silhouetted against sunset's purple sky. I thought it was Jonah. It seemed unlikely it would be any other crow come visiting. It tapped on the window again and cocked its head. It wanted me to let it in.

I didn't move. Staring back at it, I shook my head.

That sent it into an angry frenzy. It tapped on the glass, so hard I thought it would crack the thin pane. I looked away, and that made it angrier. I stared at the wallpaper, tracing the pattern of green leaves, faded now, and the even more faded yellow flowers, so pallid they were almost imperceptible, and pretended I didn't know it was there.

I sat down on the bed, which squeaked conversationally underneath me then fell silent. I folded my hands in front of me and stared down at them. Long-fingered hands, strong hands. Hands that had flown me through shells and explosion and death.

They fell into the shape of prayer without my even thinking about it.

Father McNeill and Sister Madonna would have approved. They would have told me that if I talked to God, he would listen. All my prayers would be answered, and that was good, even if it was in a mysterious way that you couldn't understand at the time but which unraveled itself into meaning years later.

But I had talked to God many times, until his reply had been far too mysterious for me. Death was a shitty answer to a prayer. That betrayal still burned at me, as fresh and bitter tasting as yesterday.

I missed my friend Jesus. I used to think of him as someone I could talk to. I carried on a conversation in my mind, addressed to him, and I never worried that he wasn't listening or didn't want to hear what I was saying.

I'd put that away the day the captain died, the day he and God betrayed me.

I wondered if Jonah would hurt himself, the way he was squawking and flapping. I raised my head and said, not out loud but in my head: I won't compromise myself. Take me as I am, but not any other way.

I felt the silence listening. The way Jesus used to listen.

I said, Take it or leave it.

A rap again at the window.

Maybe that was my answer. Vile creature of a viler God, a God of poison and birdshit, of malicious eyes and sooty feathers.

Let him come in, then, and give me my answer.

When I swung the window open, he exploded in at me, a wrath of feathers and squawks. Instinctively I flailed and swatted, using all my strength.

He hit the wall with a thump and a noise, quiet as a twig snapping, as his neck broke.

But he was still alive. The angry beads of his eyes glittered as he lay, a feathery lump whose only motion was the in and out of its breaths. A line of sunset-orange light played over his belly and fingered a crack in the wall, awaking an answering glint inside.

I wrapped my hand in the pillowcase before I pulled his body away from the wall. He made a rattling sound of hatred and pain, and died.

I tugged the wall board aside to widen the crack. Inside were rings, a watch, more. A cufflink set with diamonds. A $20 gold piece with the Queen's face on it.

I felt dazed, wrapped in cotton wool that kept the world away from me, perceived through a layer of confusion or in a darkened mirror.

God had answered my prayer.

Or had he? Was the world so random that none of this meant anything?

Either everything is random, or God's hand moves all the pieces, including me, and Father McNeill, and the Doctor, and Jonah. A God who calculates things so precisely that when a bird falls, you see the last trace of sunlight answering you. Setting you free. A patient God waiting for something so large that Jonah and I were unimportant cogs. Maybe that God calls upon us according to our nature and doesn't care what we are, or what we call ourselves.

Tonight I'm leaving. Rappaccini has looked for Jonah all day, calling and calling, but he hasn't thought to search the grounds yet. Eventually he will.

I've packed the few supplies I have. They'll take me over the mountains, I think, into the sun.

I have a traveling companion, an old acquaintance. He's invisible, inaudible. I don't know what he wants, precisely. Maybe he's a figment. Maybe he's not.

But if I think he's there, it comforts me. And there is so little comfort in this world.

Afternotes:

A protagonist who is handicapped, Native American, and transgendered is not an easy pick, but this one wanted his story told. The story began in watching a crow and thinking about how we almost always portray intelligent animals as benign. What would happen, I wondered, with a sociopathic crow who happens to team up with a fellow-minded human?

Some readers will notice the reference to Nathaniel Hawthorne's "Rappacini's Daughter," one of my favorite stories as an early reader.

HER WINDOWED EYES, HER CHAMBERED HEART

FRENZIES OF GINGERBREAD ADORNED the house's facade, but it was splintery, paint peeling in long shaggy spirals that fuzzed the fretwork's outlines. The left side of the house drooped like the face of a stroke victim, windows staring blindly out, cataracted with the dusty remnants of curtains.

Agent Artemus West thought that it would have given a human man the chills. He glanced back at Elspeth to see how she was taking it, but her face was chiseled and resolute as a fireman's axe.

"You all right?"

She swabbed at her forehead with a bare forearm, leaving streaks of dark wet dirt. "Thank your lucky stars you're mechanical and don't feel the heat," she rasped.

Hot indeed if enough to irritate her into mentioning that. He chose to ignore it.

The house sagged amid slumping cottonwoods, clusters of low-lying trees, their leaves ovals of green and pale brown. Three stories, and above that, two cupolas thrust upward into the sky, imploring, the left one tilted at an angle. The wind whistled through the fretwork, a shifting, hollow sound, like a jug's mouth being blown across. There had once been a flower garden towards the back. Weeds had claimed most of it, but the papery red heads of poppies blazed among the tangle. The sky stretched high and blue and hollow overhead.

His spurs jingled as he clanked up the front steps. His eyes ratcheted over the scene for clues, but it was clear that their fugitive had entered by the front door, which hung a few inches ajar.

Wood creaked under Elspeth's slower treads. "This was his mother's house," she said.

She'd gone over the files meticulously as always, then summed up the details for him as they'd ridden along. He ticked through them in his head. "The scientist?"

"Angeline Stoddard Eisenmacher, yes. She helped discover how to harness phlogiston. She was working in Seattle for the war effort. Then she retired out here when she got lungrot and lasted another two years."

Phlogiston, the most precious material in the world, capable of fueling marvelous machines like himself. Artemus carried a scraping of it, small as a fingernail clipping, deep in his midsection. Once a year, it was replaced, but it was valuable enough that he'd had people try to kill him for it before.

So far none had succeeded. And if it seemed that someone was about to, he held, secret in another internal pocket a sliver of terra fluida, a substance that, when combined with phlogiston, would explode. He would do that rather than be taken.

"Think he knows we're here?"

"Of course he does," she said. "But where else will he go? We've hunted him through the Deadlands and then the Cascades." She glanced back along the trampled swathe they had made coming through the sea of grass. In these plains, trees were evidence of water; this cluster of cottonwoods was an oasis in this semi-desert.

Artemus doubted the man would try to escape. No, he'd try to hide himself in the house well enough to convince them that he was no longer there, in the hopes they'd move along.

But while Eisenmacher might have some inkling of Artemus's nature, he didn't realize how implacable the mechanical man could be. When your brain is made of a network of magnets and wires, it doesn't feel boredom the same way impermanent human flesh does.

Or perhaps he overestimated Artemus by thinking him capable of giving up in the first place.

Elspeth said, "Angeline Eisenbacher worked on devices like you."

He paused. "Do you think there are any in the house?"

"I do," she said. "I looked at her invoices, from after she arrived here. She was working on something."

"That must be what her son is after. A device that can protect him." If he had been human, he might have been irritated.

As he stepped towards the door, it slammed shut.

The night before they arrived at Eisenmacher's house, Artemus had laid counting the number of stars stretched out across the sky like a sequined shawl and listened to the sound of Elspeth's breathing. Twice he heard it quicken, as though she were running through nightmares. Each time he considered rising and going to her, laying his hand on her shoulder to quell whatever monsters were chasing her, but her breathing shifted back before he ever moved.

In the early morning, as the sky began to lighten, she woke as she always did, all at once, eyes opening. One swipe of her hand across her face, and she was ready for the day. It was remarkable. He knew no women like her, even among her fellow female Pinkerton agents.

On the other hand, he rarely socialized with humans. He was the Pinkerton Agency's equipment, and equipment didn't socialize in the evenings, didn't go out to the opera or to a friend's house. It sat in a storeroom instead.

Elspeth was assigned to make sure nothing happened to him. That was her main purpose and had been for the last two years.

Humans were odd. Sometimes when their thoughts ran in the same track over and over, they could no longer think of anything else. That was, he calculated, what had happened to her. She had become obsessed with him.

Not for the first time, he thought that it would be best for her if she were to find another assignment.

He didn't know why he'd never told his superiors that.

She heated water in the last of the coals to make tea and wash her face, then ate a handful of dry biscuits from her saddlebag.

"We have time," he said. "You can make yourself a better breakfast if you like."

She shook her head. "Let's get this over." She didn't like these missions, he knew. They'd argued them over the campfire more than once. She thought it wrong to make someone into a clank against their will. And that they couldn't be trusted once they had been converted into their new mechanical form.

Still, the clanks produced from their missions, the injured men made healthy again by the addition of mechanical limbs and other appurtenances, those were an important part of the war effort, the effort that had been going on almost two decades now.

The man they were chasing had given up any say in the matter when he had shot a hospital guard dead and then climbed out a window to escape. They would capture him, and he would be taken back to the War Hospital for the series of operations that would make him a mechanical soldier.

Artemus was not like those soldiers. He had never been human, had no memories of flesh or love. He had been created by the English scientist, Patrick Lovelace, only eight years ago. The first few of those he spent idyllically, living with his master as a companion, entertaining guests with the marvels of calculation and conversation that he could perform. But when Lovelace had fallen on hard times, he had offered Artemus up to the Pinkertons, who had readily perceived the advantages of a mechanical detective.

They stared at the closed door.

"Should we look for another way in?" Elspeth asked. Her voice was uneasy, not a natural intonation for her. Artemus had seen her face down wild bears, men with guns, and even once a werewolf. He looked at her now. She shook herself like a dog shedding water and returned the glance, one fine blond eyebrow raised in question.

"If it were still open, I would say yes," he told her. "But if the door is shut, that's not how they want us to come in."

"They?"

He shrugged. "Maybe just he. But let's not make any assumptions beforehand."

The door was locked, he found when he tested it. The ornate lock was a thing of chambers and barrels and prongs, but it took him only a few moments to figure out how to spring it.

He pushed it open, though he made sure he wasn't standing directly in the doorway as he did so. A bullet wouldn't damage him the way it would a human, but it could still hit a delicate mechanism or intricate joint. The hinges cried out as the door moved slowly inward.

They crouched on either side of the opening, listening hard, before he nodded and stepped inside, Elspeth following seconds afterward.

They stood in the middle of what had once been a formal parlor, full of graceful wooden furniture whose stuffed cushions were ragged tufts now, horse hair and batting stolen by mice for generations of nests. A cuckoo clock hung askew on the gray wallpaper scrolled with black fleur-de-lis. On the wall opposite them, shelves built into the wall housed books, but when Artemus pulled one out from the leather-bound array, it fell to pieces in his hand, bookworms wriggling frantically away across the shredded carpet's gaps.

"How long has this place been deserted?" he asked.

"A decade." Elspeth's face was pale. Like most Pinkerton agents, she had a touch of the Sight. "Something's wrong. It shouldn't be like this."

"Could something else have taken it over?" Empty spaces drew supernatural creatures.

She shook her head but didn't answer. Her shoulders stooped as though she struggled to stand up.

"Elspeth?" He made a question of her name.

"She doesn't want us here."

"His mother?" But ghosts were easy to dispel with salt and iron. A ghost wouldn't make her look like that. But even so, she nodded.

"Angeline Eisenmacher is still here?"

"No and yes." Her eyes were bewildered. "I can't tell you more than that."

Through an open archway, they could see the dining room, a massive table leaning dizzily on a broken leg, surrounded by crouched chairs, like lions feeding on a kill. The paintings on the wall were scenes of mountains that Artemus, checking the almost encyclopedic memory Doctor Lovelace had installed, thought might be the Lusitanians.

A cuckoo clock hung near another door that most probably led to the kitchen. They chose not to investigate the apparently empty room, but chose the other archway, which led to a hallway winding its way deeper into the house. The carpet underfoot was also mouse-chewed, and all of the pictures hung askew or fallen, only a cuckoo clock hanging intact.

Elspeth said, "That's the third clock like that."

Artemus examined the clock. It seemed unremarkable: a typical Bavarian clock, once bright colors now faded. "It's ticking," he said. "Eisenmacher must've wound it."

He touched the dial. Immediately the cuckoo's door slid open and a fierce beak stabbed out at his fingers.

As he withdrew them, the beak's owner appeared in the doorway and then launched itself into the air: a tiny clockwork bird, no bigger than a hummingbird. It hovered in the air, regarding them, the air shrilly protesting the rapid beat of its wings.

They both stood stock still, waiting. Artemus estimated the distance between himself and Elspeth, in case the bird dove at her. Those metal wings looked razor sharp.

But after a moment, the bird buzzed away and down the corridor.

"Still some life in the house, it seems," Artemus observed.

As they explored the first floor, other birds emerged from the cuckoo clocks that seemed to have been mandatory for every room. Most swooped away as the first one had, but several began to follow the pair at a distance.

Artemus kept listening. Somewhere in this house was the fugitive Eisenmacher, perhaps listening in turn, trying to figure out where they were. He could hide in one place and stay there, if the hole were deep and hidden enough, or he might rely on moving around the house in synchronicity with their movement, hiding only where they had already looked. But, if the latter, Artemus would hear him.

Instead, all he heard were the hum of the birdwings and the small noises of breath and heartbeat and motion that Elspeth made, and the creaks and murmurs of the house answering her.

They found little but dust and spider webs and decaying furniture in the rooms they passed through at first. Then they began to find traps: the trigger wire that shot a crossbow bolt through a doorway, a floor that gave way into a hole leading God knows where. A chair with knives stabbing up from its arms. A heavy glass chandelier ready to fall, right where one might pause to look out the window.

And odd things that he wasn't sure were traps. The woman who had built this house had spared no expense as far as modern conveniences went. Stove, icebox, washing machine... All just a little more advanced than they should be, improved by Eisenmacher.

He asked Elspeth, "What did she do for the war?"

She shook her head. "Classified."

That wasn't helpful.

Artemus went first always. Elspeth followed behind. They had been working together long enough that they knew each other's reactions. They made their way through a hallway that curled past the kitchen, then led towards a narrow servants' staircase.

"Eisenmacher?" Elsbeth called. They listened to her voice echoing through the rooms upstairs. "This is pointless, sir. Come out and save us all a lot of time."

A voice echoed from somewhere. Artemus spun, but he couldn't figure out where it was coming from. "Go back, Pinks! I won't go with you, dead or alive."

And then the house began to come to life.

※

It started with the gaslights flickering in the manner of all gaslights, but they were the wrong color. They were white with just a hint of brilliant blue, the color of phlogiston. Birds buzzed through the air, a whirling crowd of clockwork. Upstairs, faint music played: a tinny, old-fashioned waltz.

One by one, every window snapped shut, then each door except for one, directly facing them: the doorway framing narrow wooden stairs, proceeding upward, then twisting around so you couldn't see what stood at the head of the stairs. The birds subsided.

Artemus and Elspeth exchanged glances. Elspeth's hands moved in sign language.

He wants us to go upstairs. That seems like a good reason not to.

Artemus replied, But how else will we catch him?

It's a trap.

Traps are most effective when the prey isn't wary. He's bitten off more than he chew.

Doubt crawled across her face but she nodded reluctantly.

He'd removed his spurs the night before. Now he eased his booted foot onto the first stair, not in the center but to the side where it was less likely to creak, listening for any sound of movement from above.

Step. Step. Step. He was almost to the tiny landing where the stairway turned. This was a staircase for servants, who wouldn't have been allowed to use the carpeted, wide front stairway. He wondered what had happened to the servants when Mrs. Eisenmacher died. Had they fled together, no longer willing to live in this isolated place, miles and miles from any civilized gathering? What had made Mrs. Eisenmacher seek out this spot to build a house?

And, moreover, such a grand house, like one of the mansions in Seattle, far to the west.

When he inched his head around to look up the stairs to their head, he saw no one standing there, beside the squat brass post that ended the banister. The air was still silent except for the sound of his partner's breath.

If he had been capable of pride, he would have gloried in the silence with which he could move. No clumsy, clanking machine he, but rather a carefully calibrated mechanism.

He was almost to the top of the stairway. The quiet air felt thick, as though it had congealed with time. Behind him, Elspeth followed, her steps loud in his ears, even though he knew someone else would not have been able to perceive them. There was a thin gray light, stronger to one side as though coming in through the front windows of the house, only half able to enter it.

Elspeth's revelation that the house might contain others like him had given him pause. The Pinkerton agency had invested in him because he was so effective against humans. But he'd never fought other mechanicals.

He rested his palm on the top of the post and paused again, listening.

With the quickness of a striking serpent, the top of the post elongated upward into a brassy tendril, several inches wide at the base then tapering slowly into a metal tentacle. It coiled around his wrist with a pressure that would have sheared a human hand off, but only slightly indented his metallic skin. It exerted that pressure for several seconds as he tried to pull away from it, then abruptly released him. He leaned back, only his inhuman speed allowing him to avoid its slash out through the air towards his face.

Elspeth had stepped backwards, down in order to avoid its reach, a pistol in her hand. The brass tentacle wavered as though trying to figure out what was going on, searched first a few inches towards him, then her. Elpseth's gun tracked the movement, but she held her fire, letting him act.

This time he was prepared. His hand flashed out to grab the tentacle at its base and pull with all his strength. Metal screeched protest as it detached from the rest of the post, and oily blue fluid gushed like blood from the jagged stump. The tentacle writhed wildly in his grasp, spraying more fluid across the stairs.

Elspeth teetered on the suddenly slick stairs, leaning sideways. With horror, he saw a panel slide open to catch her flailing figure, then shut again.

He was down the stairs in an instant, hammering on the panel. Wood splintered, but behind it lay an iron surface.

"Elpseth!" he shouted, and listened, but no answer came, only fresh laughter from the second floor.

He struck the iron once with all his strength, which sounded like a gong throughout the cavernous house.

A bird swooped close and his hand flashed out. It hadn't understood the speed he was capable of; it tried to dodge but his hand closed around it, imprisoning it. Its beak flashed out, striking at his fingers, leaving fine lines where it had scored the metal skin, but it could not escape.

He looked down at it. His fingers started to tighten, to crush it, but he relented.

It was like himself, something made and yet alive.

He opened his hand and it flickered away, to where two other birds hung in the air, out of reach. They watched him as they hovered, but made no other move.

All he could do was go on.

The source of the laughter could not be found on the second floor, no matter how he searched. It echoed through the vents, bouncing and re-bouncing until there was no way to figure out where it was coming from.

He searched meticulously, disarming trap after trap, and the thought came to him that he was moving faster now than he could have if he had had his partner in tow. But the advantage of speed was not something he would have sacrificed her for.

There was only one staircase leading to the third floor, its narrow confines showing that it was reserved for servants and storage. He hesitated at its foot. He did not have a sense of smell in the way that humans did, but he was capable of analyzing impure air. Something up there was long dead.

Surely that smell would have kept his quarry from going that way. But he went upstairs nonetheless, cautiously skirting anything that might behave as the post had.

He discovered the servants remained.

He discovered the servants remained.

There were five of them, not an unusual number for a house the size. They had been killed in their beds, killed with a blade that had stabbed downward with inhuman ferocity. The bodies lay in pieces, scattered like a macabre puzzle.

Thoughts bubbled in his metal brain. Had Elspeth already met such a fate? The notion made him feel very strange. She had trusted him. She had trusted him to take care of her. She had trusted him so much and so often, and he had failed her once already. He could not do that again.

He hadn't known what was going on when it first started. They had been traveling together for several months at that point. He liked her better than the first partner he'd had, who had treated him always like a machine. She acted as though he was a person and it wasn't a pretense. She really did think of him as a person.

Too much so, it turned out.

He hadn't understood the language of glances and sighs. He'd seen her watching him, but he hadn't known what lay underneath that stare.

And when she'd confessed her love, stammering and red-faced, as aware as he that this was not supposed to happen, that was when he had failed her. Human hearts were delicate; he hadn't known how to reject her without breaking hers.

How could he love her? His brain wasn't constructed for such things.

She'd never spoken of it again since that night.

Neither had he. He wanted to. He wanted very badly to talk about it. Time and time again, he'd thought of somehow raising it once more. But after that, her eyes were closed to him and while they spoke as partners, it was different than how they'd spoken before.

Now she was helpless, and even possibly dead. They'd give him a new partner and he'd go back to being a machine rather than a person.

He examined the bodies but did not touch them other than to close the upward staring sockets. He moved through the rooms, wondering what had happened. Then something nudged at his thoughts. He flickered through his mind, examining what he'd seen of the house so far, constructing a model of it within his brain.

There. There was a hidden room on the third floor.

He thought he'd have to smash through the walls, and worried that again he would find obdurate iron. But once he looked, the secret catch was easy enough to find.

Birds clustered, watching him.

Would he find the fugitive inside?

Then the door swung open fully, and he realized he had found an Eisenmacher, but not Richard. Rather, his mother.

She sat in a wicker chair by the window staring out, wrapped in blankets, so mounded that the fine silvery white hair on her head was barely visible.

The rest of the room was a sprawl of papers and tools and cogs and gears, cluttering the two long tables. Bookshelves lined the walls, more books crammed in them than they could gracefully hold.

Angeline Eisenmacher did not move as he walked over to her. As he approached, he realized why.

She was dead.

The patch of sunlight her chair sat in had come and gone, come and gone, over the decade, baking her dry and withered. He reached out to touch her shoulder.

At that slight contact, she crumbled away, falling into dry brown dust and a scattering of hair. The blankets slumped. At the same time, there came a vast windy noise, an anguished sound so loud it drove him to his knees, trying to cover his ears.

It died away slowly, ebbing with slight resurgences, a sound like human sobbing.

"Noooooooooooooo!" A force crashed into him from behind and sent him sprawling still dazed from the sound.

Eisenmacher. The man was striking him with doubled fists, blows bouncing off Artemus' chest. Tears streaked the man's cheeks, and Artemus tried to be gentle as they grappled, catching the man's wrists in his unbreakable grip.

"Where's my partner?" he demanded. But Eisenmacher seemed not to hear him, only sobbing and trying to pull away, pulling in the direction of the crumpled blankets, the drift of bones and dust. Artemus let go. The man posed no threat.

Released, Eisenmacher lurched over to the chair, falling in front of it on his knees to bury his head where his mother's lap might once have been.

"My partner," Artemus repeated.

Eisenmacher raised his head, looked at him with glassy eyes. "What?"

"The woman who was with me. Where is she? Where did you take her?"

"I didn't take her," Eisenmacher said.

Artemus frowned. "One of your mother's automatons?"

"Her what?"

"Did she make guards?"

Eisenmacher gazed at him until realization began to dawn. He threw his head and brayed out a surge of jagged laughter that collapsed into gasps. "Her automatons? Do you think she would have spent the last years of her life on something as petty as that?" He gestured around himself. "Don't you understand by now?"

Artemus took a step forward, raised a fist in threat. "Tell me!"

"The house," Eisenmacher said. "The house has taken her."

The shutters over the window slammed shut, plunging them into darkness.

"It's taken all of us," Eisenmacher's voice said.

Artemus felt his way along the wall till he reached the secret door, but when he pulled at it, it didn't open. He groped through his pockets for the supplies he carried purely for Elspeth's benefit: a tin of Congreve matches.

He struck it alight and it sizzled ablaze.

He was alone in the room.

❦

He sat down at a table and began to sort through Angeline Eisenmacher's notes.

They were scattered, disorganized, but he could see from them how brilliant she'd been, how ideas had come to her, too many to imagine, most of them entirely unrealized. This knowledge would be worth a fortune.

If he could find Elspeth and escape with it.

He'd hoped for a schematic of the house, but Angeline must have stored that elsewhere. Still, from her scattered notes, he gleaned that the house was a prototype, a brain much like his own, also powered by phlogiston, but on a vaster scale. She'd planned even grander things, vast mechanical behemoths that could stride across the battlefield, crushing everything in their path.

He found mention of the birds as well. An abandoned experiment in splitting the brain among a hundred components. Together, the birds were supposed to have the equivalent of his own intelligence, and like himself, be capable of learning from experience over time. But Angeline had been forced by the War Ministry to put them aside, in favor of the larger project. Letters back and forth revealed the War Ministry's fading enthusiasm, though. Finally, a letter signed "regretfully" terminated her association.

Her death had prevented the delivery of the project that would have vindicated her.

Setting the papers aside, he considered what to do next. He knew where Eisenmacher had gone, for the plans for this room, at least, were included in the papers. They had also revealed where the brain was located. As far away from him as possible right now, deep in the cellar. He could try to fight his way back down the stairs, or he could follow Eisenmacher through the secret chute.

It only took a few seconds to find the latch. The panel slid open, and he looked down the dark passageway. Surely it had been intended as an escape route, rather than some more ordinary use, like a laundry chute. He could only see a few feet down, but it slanted, rather than plunging.

What choice did he have? He climbed in.

He was able to control his descent. Though the metal walls were slick and provided no handhold, the confines were narrow enough that he could brace himself against the sides. But then, about the time he calculated he had reached the level of the first floor, the floor gave way under him and he found himself plummeting.

He landed on gritty stone floor, in a narrow circular room. A feeble illumination came from the outline of the only door. He moved quickly to it, testing it. Barred from the outside, and again made of iron too thick for him to break through.

"What are you?"

The voice seemed to come from nowhere at first, but then he glimpsed a small hole near the ceiling, only a few inches wide. A speaking tube of some sort.

"I'm a Pinkerton agent."

"No. What are you?"

"I'm something someone made. Like you."

"Did I make you?"

Did the house somehow think it was Angeline Eisenmacher? "No. Patrick Lovelace made me."

"What do you want here?"

"I'm here to apprehend the fugitive Richard Eisenmacher. He's wanted for murder."

The reply deafened him, a blast of sound that seemed impossibly loud coming from the tiny hole. "Noooooooooooo!"

He tried to recover. "Just let the woman and I leave." They could come back later. It was clear Eisenmacher wouldn't be leaving.

"She will stay. She will marry my son, and we will be a family again. There will be children. There will be children, and I will serve them and make more of myself to serve them."

He battled for some way to reply, and it quickly came to him. "She's more than just a breeding machine. I would think you would understand her struggle. There are very few women among the Pinkertons." Had the house absorbed enough of Angeline's personality to share her suffragist leanings?

No reply, only a cold implacable silence.

He explored his surroundings, and consulted the representation of the house in his mind. But here there were no secret doors.

The sound of scraping from the tube caught his attention. As he stared up at it, he could see movement.

A clockwork bird emerged, followed by another, then another and another. When there were a dozen or so, they hung in a cloud before him, there wings whining.

Were they trying to communicate somehow? Perhaps they were afraid if they came too close they might be caught. He lowered his hands to his sides, trying to look harmless.

The birds swooped closer, surrounded his head in a whirl of movement.

He could hear words inside his head. Were they somehow interacting with the magnetics of his brain to produce them?

Too long too long too long here, they sang inside his head.

"Can you help me escape?" he whispered, afraid that the house would hear him.

Too thick the door, too heavy. Will you help us nonetheless?

"Help you how?"

Too long too long too long here, will you set us free, will you set her free?

Now he understood what they were asking

He didn't know how long it took him to think it through. The house would build others like itself it had said. He thought of the war behemoths, thought of them marching towards Seattle.

He thought of Elspeth, captive. Thought about her smile. Thought about the words that had engraved themselves on his brain, "I know it's crazy and impossible, but I love you."

Thought about her, held captive to produce children.

I know it's crazy and impossible, but I love you.

⁂

He had never opened the compartment in his chest before. It surprised him how small the strand was.

He said to the birds, holding it out, "Put it in her brain and you will be free."

If that hidden brain was powered by the amount of phlogiston he thought it was, the explosion would take out the entire house.

He sat back down, and thought about Elspeth, and waited to die.

⁂

The door opened. Elspeth stood there. He gaped at her.

"Hurry," she said." We've got to escape before she realizes the mistake she made."

They fled up a narrow, iron-runged stair, which rang like a gong beneath their steps. There was no sign of the birds. How long did they have?

Emerging in the kitchen, they battered themselves against the shutters, to no avail.

Then a cloud of birds, a rush of birds, hundreds of tiny bodies flinging themselves against the window, splintering and falling as they shattered, and the window crashed open.

Artemus flung Elspeth out first, followed after her, grabbed her hand, and said, "Run!"

They ran. There was a great thundering roar behind them as the house exploded, and a hand of heated air pushing them forward even faster.

And then the sound of the house falling in on itself, and the crackle of flames.

When they finally turned to watch it, Artemus said, "How?"

The distant flames tinted her skin pink and red. "She thought I was accepting my fate. I told her if I was to be mistress of the house, I needed the keys to the pantry and all the rooms, like a proper housewife."

Perhaps the house had wanted so badly to think that its desires would be realized, that it had accepted her words. No matter what, it had underestimated Elspeth in a way that Artemus thought the original Angeline might not have.

The horses were gone, frightened away by the explosion. It would be a long journey across the mountains to Seattle, but they'd endured worse before, and surely they would encounter some help along the way.

As they turned their back on the house, Artemus didn't see the several small fluttering forms, exiting from the ashes and debris.

As he walked, he reached out and took Elspeth's hand. She hesitated, then twined her fingers through his.

They went on, the birds following after them.

Afternotes:

This story came from a fondness for a particular episode of the television show, Wild West West, called "The Night of the House."

WEB OF BLOOD
AND IRON

THE HOTEL PUT MANSERVANTS and maids up in their own rooms, one attic below the hotel staff: housekeepers, valets, clerks, kitchen staff. The manager lived on-site as well, his family taking up half the floor below that, and I'd heard his children, happily shrieking, more than once in the pool or playing tag in the stairwells.

I wouldn't have minded a room to myself, but instead I was sleeping on a cot in his Lordship's suite, down on the third floor. I was lying there enjoying the Cannes sounds of birds and street bustle and funeral rumble of the trains and reading when I heard the door fumbled open and his lordship lurching in.

Alive for another day.

I was up cat-quick, and went in to help him off with his tuxedo, ripe with boozy sweat and cigar smoke and the hyacinth scent the siren whores wear. He was so drunk I was surprised he'd made it home at all, that none of the vampire gamblers had decided to take him home for a nightcap instead of selecting a whore.

He chattered away to me as I sponged his forehead. He always slept nude. Every lycanthrope I'd served – and I've served six so far of his Lordship's family, the deVulfs – has shared that trait.

"Made enough to keep us here another week," he said with a grin.

I doubted that, given the size of his weekly liquor tab. I took care of his bills as well, so his ideas of money were usually far off the mark. But his father would supplement that well enough that we could stay.

His cleaning bill was as large as my wages, and I'm better paid than most. The Yorkshire coal mines made the De Vulffs a lot of money.

The question was not how long he could stay. Rather, it was how much longer till one of the vampires discovered his ruse?

I decided to save that for a later argument, when he would be soberer, though.

Stubble sprouted on his chin a mere hour after each time I'd shaved him with the bone and steel razor so I didn't bother now to do more than wipe his face. He could go to sleep shaggy and untroubled, smelling only of wolf.

We gnomes have senses almost as acute as theirs. It's one way we read the earth: metal tang and mineral salts, loam and chalk and bland sandy stone.

He fingered his wrist, where the silver charm was soldered to an iron band.

"You still want to leave, don't you?" he asked me, voice harsh.

"I think it would be wisest, sir," I said without looking at him. "We could drive up along the coast, swing through Paris, then Calais, be at your club for dinner and some good mutton."

He huffed out amusement. "Appealing to my animal appetites."

"Appealing to your common sense," I said, meeting his eyes this time.

They shifted from brandied amusement to muted chocolate sadness. "Not until I know what happened to Delarieve."

"She wouldn't have wanted you to endanger yourself."

He turned away, fists bunched at his side. "I know one of those bastards can tell me what happened to her. Whether she's still alive. My father still has enough influence that they listen to me."

Maybe. But I didn't say that aloud. While the vampires held social ascendancy right then, it was true they hadn't always, and at one point had reckoned the opinions of the werewolves into their choices. But I didn't think his title would prevent them from tearing his throat out if – perhaps even just when – they discovered he'd been cheating for two weeks now. The charm's silver burned at him, but it would ward off any vampire's touch. But that was a flimsy defense – if it happened to slide out from beneath his cuff, any vampire looking at it would know it for the cheating luck charm it was.

He padded over to his bed and collapsed on it, sprawling on his stomach.

I pulled the sheet over him and went to go prepare his evening clothes for yet another night before returning to the pages I'd been wading through, Marx's *Critique of Hegel's Doctrine of the State*.

Delarieve. I'd been tired of her from the very beginning, but no servant gets to pick who his or her master falls in love with. An American girl with delusions of following in the footsteps of Nellie Bly or Jennie June. A war correspondent, here in Europe to cover the wars and convulsions. Back in the States, they'd preserved their freedom, to a degree. Here the vampires, fairies, and their ilk owned the continent, had ever since they'd stepped in to end the World War.

What would have happened if they hadn't? Who's to say it would have been as bad as they claimed?

He'd met Delarieve in London. Mixing with a human was bad enough, but when she'd gone off to the French Riviera in search of some story, he had told her he'd meet up with her. But before he'd managed the preparations, she'd stopped answering his letters.

I hoped that she'd simply found someone else, some other wealthy pigeon to pluck. But given how she'd vanished out of sight, I thought it might well be the wrongdoing that lord Mark believed it to be.

Two weeks now without much clue. People had seen her. But ask where she had gone, and they looked vacant, unknowing.

Out in the courtyard, Jean asked if I wanted the Delahaye brought round, as he had every day, and as always, I shook my head. But I went into the garage to see it nonetheless, as though it were a horse I meant to comfort. It sat there in the shadows, which washed out the robin's egg blue of its sides, turning them gray. Sleek and ready. My favorite of all his lordship's cars, barely two months off the assembly line.

I ran my palm over the silver of its trim, wishing I had some reason to drive it away now.

Wishing I had some reason to leave altogether. That the courage of my convictions would let me leave his lordship, the foolish child of an unfair class system, behind.

But despite all my feelings about the aristocracy – as Marx said, their parasitic nature had always existed, even before the vampires had claimed them – whenever I looked at Mark, I saw him as the boy he had once been, full of fancies abut knights and chivalry and quests.

He might not acknowledge it right now, but that was what he was doing right now, being a perfect knight riding off to rescue his damsel.

I hoped she appreciated it. At least, that she was alive to do so.

⚜

By six PM, his lordship was up and ready to be shaved and dressed. I had sandwiches sent up, something to tide him over till he went out. There were shadows under his eyes as though he hadn't slept.

"Where to tonight?" I asked as I stirred the lather, smelling of bay rum, and spread it over the black shadows on his jawline.

"Jenkins," he said. "He's set up some sort of game in his car on the train. Says it will be novel."

"Novel" is not a word one likes to hear from an older vampire. So often their ideas of novelty involve pain.

And of course a train. The vampires were obsessed with the trains. Before their occupation, travel had been idiosyncratic: carriages and the occasional automobile. Now their trains thundered through the night, every night, great black things whose whistles called back and forth like hunting hawks, a network of iron connecting every city and town in this area, always spreading, a spiderweb claiming this country and all beyond it.

"Have the front desk call me a taxi." My lord studied his lapels, fingering the wide black expanse, before he held out an arm and I placed his watch, freshly wound, on his wrist. Gold, not silver. A showy piece, but one vampires would appreciate. They like gaudy on other people.

He looked at me. "Do you want to come, Toby?"

He hadn't asked me that before. It wouldn't be anything new to have me there waiting on him while he gambled, but previously I'd avoided the vampires. They like nonhuman blood more than human and they're not hesitant about feeding on servants. Would his presence keep me safe?

But there were tired blue shadows under his eyes. He needed backup. He needed a friend there.

His servant would have to do.

He didn't speak in the taxi, just stared out with knitted brows. Already stubble shadowed his jaw, and his Adam's apple worked as he swallowed.

Not my place to speak, so I stared out the opposite window, running through my inventory. A good manservant is always supplied, from the mints and handkerchiefs in my waistcoat to the Bangalore Torpedo, all chambers loaded, secured along my calf to match the dagger's weight on the other side.

When we pulled up at the station, I fell in line behind him, my boots crunching along the gravel. Jenkins – Lord Jenkins, the Earl of Westumber, to be precise – had a private train, resting on a side track right now. The only other train was Le Train Bleu, getting ready to depart in a few minutes. Not one of the new vampire trains, but the old passenger train, elegant and appointed, carrying passengers in true continental style. The air smelled of coal smoke and sea brine.

He still didn't talk as we walked towards the car but I could see him preparing himself, squaring his shoulders, putting on his fatuous face, a simple English werewolf interested in a little gambling and a lot of drink. All surface.

A sleek fellow, hair slicked back and smelling of Cassie pomade, fell into step beside his Lordship. "Fine evening," he drawled. The slight slurring betrayed him as vampire; they prefer not to hide their teeth, no matter what.

Beside me, the vampire's Renfrew, a silent servant like myself. I stole a sidelong glance: human, far-gone, staring straight ahead.

Inside, cigar and incense smoke tinged the air blue and battled it out for supremacy, ending in a tie. A subdued clink of crystal and cutlery, the ruffle of cards, the clatter of dice, came from the various tables scattered throughout the room, augmented by the murmur of voices. Vampires almost always speak softly. I've always thought it a way of demonstrating their power – forcing listeners to strain their ears is more effective than shouting sometimes.

The sleek man tugged his Lordship over to a table; the Renfrew and I moved to the antechamber filled with other servants. No one spoke there. The Renfrews stared ahead silently; the two others, myself and a harried looking human, exchanged glances. Everything was hushed as velvet, opulent and curlicued.

We stood there silently, pretending to be furniture, as the gamblers played. Now and then a player would signal, and his servant would dart out from the crowd, wipe his brow, fetch a new drink, or whatever other small service was necessary.

My lord's table was nearby, a cluster of vampires and him, sitting like a terrier amid a crowd of smiling cats. I couldn't hear them at first, but I subtly nudged my way through the crowd to stand nearer. None of the Renfrews objected, though one sneered at me as I shouldered past him and another smiled and licked his lips at me, a sneaky little taunt that would have earned him a punch in the face out in the street.

Three of the vampires at the table were of little account: hangers on, the inconsequential scum at the edge of this pond. But the vampire my Lord sat across from was Wilfrid von Blodam.

Von Blodam was slight, and blonde, turned at an age when his trim little blonde beard was barely past peachfuzz. He dressed immaculately, expensively, and had not one servant in attendance, but two, a pair of matched twins, who stood ready to anticipate any need. He was the most powerful vampire in Cannes, and was rumored to be working his way up the power chain as the vampires solidified their hold on the continent.

Before they spread out over the world, I thought, and then thrust that thought away as quickly as I could. Some of them are telepaths.

But how can any of us avoid thinking about the covert war? Great Britain, where the fairy strongholds are based, holds out, and the various African power groups have worked together to do so as well. And the vampires will have to work hard and long to take America, with its vast stores of phlogiston. Already the vampires have spread out so far from their origin point that some have gone eastward, beginning to nibble at Russia.

My lord signaled. I refreshed his whiskey. The air at the table felt grave-cold, despite the heat in the rest of the room, and the smoke seemed to clear around the table, rendering it a clear bubble in the hazy interior.

My Lord studied his cards.

"Do you know," von Blodam drawled, "where the little journalist went to, the American girl? I kept seeing her around the station, asking questions about the trains."

The twitch of my Lord's shoulder would have been as apparent to the vampire's keen perceptions as it was to me, who only saw it because I knew him so well.

"That one that always wore that little blue hat?" he said lightly, still studying his cards. "I was wondering that myself. Took her out for a drink and thought I'd do it again but the bitch vanished on me. No one seems to know where she went to." He glanced at me. "Don't hover, Smithers, it's damned annoying."

I retreated to my cul de sac.

Von Blodam kept playing on the theme throughout the night. "As the Commandant of this zone," he said, "I should be tracking these sorts of people better. I tell you, what, Lord de Vulff, I'll let you know if I hear anything of her."

My lord kept playing, but he was losing steadily despite the medallion at his wrist. You could practically see the money flowing through his fingers, all that labor, hours of coalmining, transmuted into coins that he spent like water, without even thinking of it.

The rich don't think themselves rich. They count themselves hard up to practice economies such as a single carriage instead of two, or foregoing buying more land or another factory to make them richer. It's easy to hate them for that, and nowhere had I seen it played out so excessively, so freely, shows of wealth that would have been vulgar if they didn't manage to subdue that quality through sheer amount. One man was beggared and dragged away after he bet what he should not have.

Von Blodam saved his taunts for when my lord was about to make decisions, and while my lord's face remained impassive, I could read the emotions there, the confusion and fury. Von Blodam wanted him to attack, I thought, wanted to taunt him into action so he'd have an excuse.

With that realization, I tried to will my lord to come away, to keep calm, tried to put my own thoughts in his head, though there wasn't a chance of that, as though through sheer force of will I could somehow make him do what he should and back away.

Cold sliced through my heart as von Blodam turned his ice blue eyes towards me, studying me like a half-dissected specimen. "Your servant came with you from England, did he not?" he asked my Lord.

My Lord's back could have been a steel rod, but his voice was leisurely. "Smith of Smithfield. Their family has been serving mine for generations now, haven't they, Smith?"

"Yes, my lord." My voice creaked from disuse. He gave me a dismissive nod before turning back to the table and pushing the conversation down a different alley. "I understand you've got one of the new Bentleys, von Blodam. How does it run?"

But von Blodam was not done with me. He beckoned, and I went to him, not looking at my lord.

"Good English gnomish blood," he mused, reaching out to trace a finger along my cheekbone. "Tell me, Smith, is there anything that would shake your faith in your master?"

"No, sir," I said. What else could I? The fingernail on my skin was dagger sharp; it sliced the flesh and I felt blood spring to it as he withdrew his hand.

"No? Nothing? But what of English honor, Mr. Smith? What if you discovered your lord had been trying to cheat at cards?"

The air pushed in on me and his eyes were like stars. I focused on my breathing.

"My lord would not do such a thing, sir," I said, forcing the words out.

"Not for money or...love?" he pressed.

"Never, sir."

He chuckled, slouching back in his chair. "Very well. Let us resume our game." The vampire beside him began to deal as I retreated.

☙❦❧

The evening wore on. Fortunes were squandered and won, and then squandered again. The cigar smoke haze thickened to the point of oppression, and the air grew stuffy except when someone entered or exited the car, bringing in a night breeze that cut through the heat like a saber stroke.

I tried to keep any thoughts from betraying us, but I could not help but wonder. The vampire knew my lord was cheating, he was threatening to say it openly, and there was only one end to it if he did make that accusation: they would kill my lord then and there.

But my lord seemed oblivious to his impending fate. He sat there playing and chattering away, an endless stream of blather that was his damned-silly-English-peer act, playing to the crowd with a touch of whimsy now and then. But underneath it all, he and I and the vampires knew, he was a werewolf, and while they had the numbers, he could at least account for some.

Lost in these thoughts, I swam back as the Renfrew beside me stepped forward to provide and light a cigarette, then retreated into his former position. My lord was talking about cars.

"Rover claims their new model goes faster than le Train Bleu," von Blodam said.

"That's nothing special," my lord asserted. "I could leave with the train from here and my car could get me to my club in London before the train hits Callais."

Von Blodam raised an incredulous eyebrow. "A bold claim."

"It's good English technology," my lord said, and the edge to his voice was the same as though he'd bared his teeth, by the way the tension jumped in the room. I felt two Renfrews sidle closer.

But von Blodam laughed. "Then perhaps we should bet on. You will race le Train Bleu, and if you win, I will give you the prize of your choice."

"And if that prize was to answer a question truthfully?" My lord's eyes burned but could not melt the room's ice.

Von Blodam smiled, and I could feel disaster looming like an iceberg. "Very well. Three questions even, answered with absolute truth, on my honor. What would you put up against something like that, my Lord?"

"Name it," said my Lord softly. "For it's clear that you are angling at something."

The toothy smile broadened. "Very well. A reward of my choice, if the train reaches Callais before you are at your club."

"A reward of your choice," my lord said.

❦

Outside, I piled him into the cab and started speaking even as the door swung close.

"What were you thinking?" I demanded. "They won't let you win."

"They don't know anything about cars," he said contemptuously. "They make their Renfrews drive them about. They won't be able to catch more than the dust we leave in our trail. And I've driven that route two, three dozen times now, half of that in the Delahaye."

He was flush with alcohol and triumph. He was young and rich and callous. How was he different, battening on the labor of honest workers, than any of the vampires?

And how could I possibly change his mind on this? No.

No, I would let him go to his fate. And, as was my hereditary place, I would accompany him.

I could do no less than that.

At 5:45 PM, we heard the whistle of le Train Bleu, departing. My lord set down his drink with a leisurely smile, saluted the watching well and ill-wishers, and sauntered over to the waiting car, gleaming in the late afternoon sunshine's warmth.

He straightened his jacket and wound a white silk driving scarf around his neck. I could have killed him. We were losing precious time.

But as soon as we were out of eyeshot of the crowd, his entire demeanour changed. "Here we go, old fellow," he said. "Hang on."

The French countryside is beautiful, they say. I caught little of it in the mad rush to Muchy Breton, where we had to search for the pharmacy in order to secure petrol. It took some amount of explaining to the clerk, who was the pharmacist's assistant, and bemused at the idea that our car would require anything at hand in his storeroom. At last, he fetched the pharmacist, who turned out to be an automobile enthusiast, with a shed full of petrol, old tires, and a blacksmith shop's worth of tools.

When I emerged, I found my lord on his knees beside the rear wheel, cursing.

"Someone's slashed the tire," he said. "Dammit all. I turned my back to go take care of a moment of natural business. Low, to stoop to that sort of behavior while a man's relieving himself."

I fumbled with the trunk and took out the spare. "And this," I said. A penknife pierced the thick rubber.

But we were in luck. I turned to the sleepy pharmacist.

The next obstacle presented itself a few miles further on. Fog covered the road, and the car swam in and out of it, a submerged salmon leaping through foamy water, curls and tendrils swirling in its wake. My lord drove slower, but barely, and more than once we swerved to avoid an incautious cow or deer. I tried not to think of how many things stood too low to be spotted through the fog.

We ascended to a hilltop and saw a basin of fog in front of us, an immense white bowl. I started to say something about the odd flapping noise that was just starting to creep up on my consciousness but before I could begin, my lord shoved me sideways, then rolled in the opposite direction himself. A massive claw flashed in the space between us and rasped against the metal before the dragon swooped back upward.

"Hold tight" We leaped down the hill and into the fog.

My lord steered with face tense, watching the road flash by mere feet from our front wheels, not slowing. Overhead we heard the flapping of the wings.

Then the hoot of a train, off to the right, somewhat ahead.

"What are you thinking, sir?" I asked. "That's not the Blue Train. It's the train to the western coast."

"I know," he said. "But the crossing is up ahead, I can hear it."

"But not see it." Fog thickened and lessened around us; sometimes I could see his resolute face, other times he was lost to me. Overhead those wings flapped, and sometimes fire coiled, once a great wash of it directly overhead accompanied by a foul, sulfurous stench. My cap had blown off my head many miles ago, and I felt the hairs atop my head singe and vanish.

"Hold tight!" my lord yelled over the roaring of the wind and if he added anything to that, it was lost in the howl of the train and the sudden flap of wings and then somehow we were soaring through space just ahead of the train, so close I could count every bar in the cowcatcher in front of it and there was a vast scream and crash as the dragon and the train collided, and then a whoosh of flame, exploding outside, that cleared the world of mist and revealed chaos.

The train, one of the great black trains, lay folded and crumpled, intermingled with the thrashing of the dragon corpse, which reminded me horribly of a chicken I had seen once with its head removed, still dashing itself against a wall in search of the escape that it was far past. The train had been pulling three vast tanks; two had broken, and black liquid was spilling out, pooling.

Or was it black? The moonlight gleamed on it as black birds swooped down, a cloud of them, the ones that had been following us, transforming into humanoid forms, to kneel beside that vast pool. We both stood, speechless, at the spectacle of the vampires lapping up the encarmined landscape, the moon glowing emptily behind their eyes.

All those trains had a hidden purpose. Carrying tanks of blood, harvested from God knew where. Not just gallons of it – an immeasurable amount.

The parasitical rich, embodied, literally drinking the blood of the poor.

"Go!" my lord said urgently, pulling me towards the car.

Reunited with the Delahaye, we hurtled through the night. My mind raced. Supplies – the trains would allow the vampires to take the world. A group of them could overwhelm a city, and the trains would let them travel any distance to do so. Despair held my heart so tight I could hardly breathe.

We made it to Calais, scrambled aboard the ferry in the nick of time. My lord did not speak all the way as we moved over the sea, and the moon made nonsensical images with the froth atop each wave.

How did von Blodam get there before us? Some trickery, or perhaps a direct train. But he did, even as we pulled up with five minutes to spare.

There was irritation in his gaze as he said, "It seems you have won, Lord von Vulff. I regret to say the French authorites intend to fine you for racing on public roads."

Amusement in his gaze, but something else…anticipation, perhaps.

"Indeed," my lord said.

"Then claim your reward." Von Blodam's teeth glinted in the moonlight.

"What happened to Delarieve?" My lord's voice was hoarse as though he had run every step of the way here.

I wanted him to be happy, despite it all. And I thought to myself, oh maybe, maybe.

"I believe you might have seen her along the way," von Blodam drawled. "Some part of her."

My lord stared at him, the beard on his cheek ragged and unkempt, his clothing in shambles from the trip's wind, as though willing him to say more.

But all the further the answer the vampire gave was not in words: he simply licked his lips and smiled as the street traffic came and went around us and we stood in the future ruins of our world.

Afternotes:

This story came from reading history, where an actual bet like this took place, although sans dragon and for considerably lower stakes.

TICKTOCK GIRL

MOMENT 20244660: SHE SITS in the front parlor, covered with white cloth. Subdued spring light washes through the folds each afternoon. Behind her in the cavernous room, the tick tock of the grandfather clock echoes, counter pointed by the steps of the servant come to wind it. The maid must be accompanied by a girl in training today; they speak in quiet, subdued tones, bringing with them the smell of soap and lemon oil.

"Spooky, that's what it is. 'Ow long has it all sat here?" The voice is high-pitched, shot through with a nervous giggle.

"Since her ladyship died. Her father ordered it all covered up, and it's sat here ever since. Going on ten years now."

"What's this now?" The dusty sheet, tugged by an inquisitive hand, slides off her face and the new maid lets out a shriek of surprise before she is quieted by the older one.

"That's the lady's mechanical woman. Used to walk and talk, they say. Still can. But her lordship said, sit here, and so she does." With a deft rustle, the sheet is tucked around her again, but as the light dims, she preserves the sight of wide blue eyes, a mouth agape in astonishment.

"Walk an' talk? Go on, yer pulling me leg."

"That's what they say. Used to march alongside her in the suffrage parades."

A cog, imprisoned in her brain, ticks, and she enters a new moment, this one left behind.

❧

Humans see time as a flow. A river, sweeping them along. But she perceives each moment, each tick and tock of the clock as a separate instance, presented as perfect as a gem inside a velvet box, each distinct minute collected within the celluloid and circuitry of her brain.

❧

Moment 1: There is something hot and hard hammering inside her chest, but perhaps that is ordinary. She has no other moments to compare this one with, here and now in the first sixty seconds of life. All that exists is the face hovering above her where she lies on a table. The features are flushed with triumph and perspiration, a mass of golden brown ringlets falling around it, one touching her brass skin.

The lips open, and sounds come out. They have meaning attached to them. "Can you hear me?"

Her own lips move. The rubber bags that are her lungs contract, squeezing out air for her tongue to shape. "Yes."

Water appears on her skin. In some other moment she will know these are Sybil's tears, but not tears of sorrow, tears of joy. There will be many kinds of tears.

"I am Lady Sybil Fortinbras," the face says. "I am your creator." Then, with a laugh, "Creatrix, I suppose."

The moment ends before she can reply.

Moment 25153800: The smell of seawater and musty cargo crates, part of so many moments, is gone. There is a long slow screech as each nail is withdrawn.

Moment 25153804: The lid comes off, and around her the packing material rustles as someone throws handfuls of it aside. Then her face is cleared and she sees him, hears his voice saying in German "A woman? What use is a mechanical woman to me? Schiesse!" He throws the last handful back and she watches it drifting down in slow motion, settling to block her sight again.

Moment 8820967: They are marching in a suffrage parade. Along High Street, hostile faces loom, shouting. She wheels Lady Sybil's chair forward. Both of them wear white dresses, sashes of purple and green. Purple for courage, green for strength. The other women ignore her. She makes them uneasy, even though she may be the only reason the crowd doesn't rush to attack them. But one, her face lean and resolute as a hatchet, leans forward to speak to Lady Sybil.

"Do you agree with what Mrs. Pankhurst says?"

Lady Sybil glances up impatiently amid the sea of white ruffles. "That the argument of the broken pane is the most valuable argument in modern politics? Perhaps. But we will work within the law. For now." Her eyes are shrewd as she looks at the people lining the street. "Why would we want the vote if we intend to go outside the bounds of the law?"

Moment 9097372: Lady Sybil is speaking. The winter has withered her even more. She is frail and fragile as a songbird.

"You see, I don't think it's enough to march anymore," she says. "There has to be some good coming from you. In this brave new age, there are villains aplenty. I'll set you after them. You have been my legs, my dear. My mechanical Athena. For so very long. And now you will be my fists."

❦

Moment 9156658: She has the dark-skinned, well-dressed man by the collar, pulling his limp form after her into the offices of Scotland Yard. She drops him in the doorway of Todd Chrisman, the detective who, she knows, has been working on the case.

"This is the Maharishi of Terjab," she says.

His eyes are amazed. "Yes, I can see that."

"He is responsible for the Soho white slave ring. You will find the evidence in his basement."

He stammers out something, moves forward to look down at the Maharishi. "What are you?" he says.

"Lady Fortinbras's mechanical Athena," she says. "My directive is to fight evildoers."

Behind him in the office, someone laughs, only to be hissed into silence by a fellow. All of these men are watching her.

❦

Moment 9230101: "This is the Dog Collar Killer," she says to Chrisman.

The man at her feet groans, recovering himself. He fought hard.

"He's a clergyman," Chrisman says, astonishment coloring his voice.

Pallid and rabbity, the man wears his robes like a squatter moved into a strange new place. He blinks, the bruises along his face coloring like dark water, and one eye weeps bloody tears.

"I am Father Jeremiah, and this is an outrage," he says, pulling himself upward despite the restraining hand on his arm.

"Marilyn Bellcastle," she says. "Lucy Stipe. Annabel Jones. He killed them all."

He explodes in spittle and anger at the sound of her voice. "Whores!" he snarls. "Jezebels! They deserved no better!"

Moment 9618905: "What have you brought us now, lass?" Chrisman asks. She gives him the papers she has compiled, the blueprints for the bomb to be placed beneath the Houses of Parliament and he thanks her, riffling through the rustling papers one by one, studying them. There are new decorations on his uniform; her aid has brought him a promotion.

Moment 9713637: Lady Sybil's father paces up and down the study, talking to himself. His cooling breakfast, the opened letter beside it, sits on the table. He wheels on her.

"Died in prison, by god!" he shouts. "Her and that Pankhust woman, thinking hunger strikes would change the gaolers' minds. What good is it dying for a stupid, frippery cause, just another chance to dress up?"

She believes this is a rhetorical question; she makes no reply. She would have been with them, but Lady Sybil felt chasing the Ghost of Belfast was more important. Chrisman should have been pleased when she brought the villain in, but he was subdued, told her simply to go home.

"I'll have every man in that prison to court," Lord Fortinbras says. He looks at her, the way he has always looked at her. Half repulsed and half proud at his clever daughter's creation.

"And you, mechanical Athena," he says. "What's to become of you now?"

There are tears on his face.

Moment 25055955: The crack of the gavel resounds through the crowded room as the auctioneer bangs the sale closed. "And sold to the foreign gentleman!"

Some of Lady Sybil's friends are there, but none of them have bid on her. She is led away to the waiting crate. She feels nothing.

⁂

Moment 49189954: Professor Delta is speaking.

"The university bought you as a historical feminist treasure," she says. "Built by an English suffragette and scientist. The once owned by Hitler stuff, that was just icing on the cake, a little thrill value. But now... nowadays people are more concerned with the rights of mechanicals than they were when you were sold."

There is a gleam in her eye that is reminiscent of the Pankhursts.

"Do you really want to be on your own?" Delta says, leaning forward. She is a short, wiry woman, her hair cropped close, no makeup on her face. "What would you do?"

"Fight crime," she says.

Delta leans back, her hand flickering in a dismissive gesture. "A superhero? Let the papers call you something like Ticktock Girl? How... trivial. It would be a terrible waste."

She could go back in the crate. But Lady Sybil built her to move. To act. To be her hands, even now.

⁂

Moment 57343680: She faces Father Jeremiah in the closed room, cinderblock walls, the smell of disinfectant harsh and immediate. Somewhere in the distance, water drips.

She's not sure how he can be alive, unchanged, a century later. But here he is.

"The Lord has preserved me! I am his Hand!" he shouts at her. She calculates the distance from her fist to his jaw, the amount of impact necessary to render him unconscious.

He draws himself up and smiles. "But you can't. I'm legit now."

The word is unfamiliar.

He splits it into syllables for her, serves it up like little rabbit pellets of words. "Le-gi-ti-mate. Everything I do is inside the law."

"You tell people to kill other people and they do it."

"All I do is provide information on where they are: the abortionists, the sodomites, the women who whore themselves out. My followers decide what to do with the knowledge."

Seeing her pause, he laughs. "Welcome to the brave new world, Ticktock, mechanical clock," he half sings. "Can't touch this, can't touch me now."

⁕

Moment 9097375: Sickness has eaten away at Lady Sybil's face, reducing it to paper over bone. But her voice is strong as ever.

"There is right and there is wrong," she says. "You, my mechanical Athena, are always on the side of right." A trembling hand strokes along the bright metal of her face. "The side of justice."

⁕

Moment 57343681 seems to blend together with so many others, so many long circles of the wheels in her brain. And in that confluence, she knows that sometimes the argument of brick and fist are the only way. Chrisman would not approve, she thinks as she snaps Jeremiah's neck. But Lady Sybil would.

Afternotes:

This is an early story that combines two loves: superheroes and steampunk. Computing the number of the moments was one of the more complicated aspects of the story.

It originally appeared in *Cyberage Adventures* and was my first chance to see an artist draw one of my characters.

Seven Clockwork Angels, All Dancing On a Pin

I F A CLOCK HAS ticked, it must tock, and thus time moves along. And
in every tick and tock, there's a story, and sometimes more than one.

Once upon a tick and tock, there was a great Lord and a greater
Lady, who were Patrons of the Arts and Sciences. They endowed libraries
and laboratories, and commissioned portraits and poems and marvelous
machines that could play chess or spin a silk thread so fine you could
barely see it or that could even build their own, tinier machines to make
tinier machines in turn, and so on and so on, until they produced the
head of a pin inhabited by seven clockwork angels, all dancing.

The Lord and Lady loved the works they commissioned, but they
yearned to produce something of their own. And one day it came to pass
that the Lady announced to her Lord that they had collaborated very well
indeed, and that she would soon produce an heir.

Their daughter was fine and fair. They named her Aurora, after the Aurora Borealis, and to celebrate her christening, they invited all the scientists and artists and musicians and philosophers and inventors they had helped.

The day of the christening, Aurora was given amazing gifts: a pair of spectacles that could see everything from the smallest cell to the farthest star; a flowering garden whose trees produced avocado pears and pineapples, cherries and peaches, all from the same branch; a clock that could tell her the time on the moon and predict the next three days' weather with reasonable accuracy; a talking parasol that recited cheerful limericks in the morning to amuse her and long, languorous epics in the evening to lull her to sleep; and sundry other delightful devices and contraptions, each more cunning than the last.

But the Lord and Lady had neglected to invite one guest, a scientist named Artemus Scuttlepinch (who might have been omitted on purpose, for he was very bad at dinner conversation) and he stepped forward at the end.

"I have a gift as well!" he announced. "Behold the Cabinet of Dreadful Fates!" He whisked his dinner cape aside with a flourish, revealing a squat box painted a malignant black. Brass dials and switches covered its face.

Scuttlepinch steepled his fingers as though preparing a classroom lecture. "I have harnessed various eldritch and magnetic energies," he said. "Whatever fate the machine pronounces for an individual, will come true, with 98% accuracy. And…" He sneered here, and would have twirled his moustache if it had been long enough. "The fates are never pleasant ones."

Before anyone could stop him, he said, "This is for Aurora!" He pressed a switch.

The machine clicked and clattered ominously, and then clicked some more, finally producing a slip of paper. Scuttlepinch snatched it up and read it aloud. "On her eighteenth birthday, Aurora will prick her finger on a spindle and die!"

"Poppycock!" shouted the Lady. "No one ever died of a pin prick!"

"Preposterous!" shouted the Lord. "The spindle is an obsolete technology!"

He signaled for the guards, who took the cackling Scuttlepinch by the arms. Another seized the machine and raising it overhead, dashed it on the ground, where it shattered, revealing a series of gleaming tubes and poisonous green lubricant, which roiled like drops of mercury on the floor. Scuttlepinch only laughed the harder; the sound sent shivers down the spines of the witnesses.

But another scientist, Miss Mariah Fleetthought, spotting Scuttlepinch, had lingered in the back of the crowd, fearing just such an occurrence. She now stepped forward, clearing her throat with a diffident manner.

"Here," she said, "perhaps this will help. My own research has led in a similar direction. This is the Good Luck Gizmo, instilled with the computational power of a Babbage engine and possessing its own chemistry of droplets distilled from wishing wells, the sap of seven leaf clovers, and another liquid whose origin I cannot disclose. It cannot avert dreadful fates, but it may alleviate them."

She set the box she held on the floor, and it unfolded into a clockwork kitten, which picked its way through the shards and droplets to leap nimbly into Aurora's crib and curl there, its green eyes glittering watchfully despite its position of repose.

After that, the Lord and Lady took comfort in the raising of their daughter and avoided thinking of her possible fate, although they were instrumental in passing a bill that banned spindles outright. She was a bright and sunny child, and their delight in her outweighed all other considerations, until the marvelous machines produced under their patronage were bundled into a cellar to sit unused and dusty.

Aurora was talented and well-tutored, and had all the social graces as well. Her only flaw, which no scientist counted an actual weakness, was a driving curiosity and a craving to know how things worked, which led to her taking many things apart before she learned how to put them back together.

In all of this, she was companioned by the clockwork cat, which haunted her footsteps and watched with wise green eyes as she dismantled things. They came to call it Gizmo, and sometimes forgot that it was not a living creature, for it seemed as cat-like as any cat, despite its devotion to the child.

On her eighteenth birthday, they held a party for Aurora, and invited many young people of her age. But she found them boring, preferring to talk to the scientists about her own discoveries and eventually, bored, she slipped away, trailed by Gizmo.

She made her way down to the cellar, where she was in the process of taking apart a particularly marvelous lace-making machine, because she was curious about the patterns it produced. Gizmo did not approve of this particular machine, which was curious, and today, as she continued to explore its inner workings, the cat grew increasingly agitated, swatting at her with a paw and meowing in its tinny voice, till she pushed it aside more roughly than she meant to.

As she did so, her balance slipped a little and her hand pushed farther into the machine, where it met a certain inner part that spun thread, something that any seamstress might have called a spindle.

She withdrew her hand with a cry of pain, looking at the drop of blood on it. Dizziness overcame her and she sat back on her heels. Darkness pressed in on her vision, but she could hear Gizmo nearby, its head pushing hard against her, purring. Her heart faltered, but the rhythm of the purrs soothed it, made it slip into a slower but still existing rhythm as she fell asleep.

Crouched beside her, the cat opened its jaws and glittering motes flew out. Anyone wearing Aurora's spectacles might have seen them: tiny clockwork angels with shining spindles, setting to work.

Bit by bit the angels spun, and the air became glass. First filling the room, suspending the sleeping Aurora, then spreading outward from the cellar, catching the mansion's inhabitants till they were suspended as well, unmoving, but still in the attitudes of life in which they had been captured: the Lord and Lady holding hands as they walked in the garden among the partygoers, looking for their daughter; the cook putting the final layer of icing on the seven-layer cake intended to cap the evening; the butler tending the enormous furnace that heated the hot-water, even the flames, all caught in glass.

Scientists came from all over to study the enormous lump of glass in the middle of the city. They tried drills of diamond and moon metal, and acids that would burn through almost anything, and certain frequencies of sound, but the glass stayed, obdurate and unyielding. Some set up camp in order to study the phenomenon; after a few decades an open-air university sprang up there, devoted to unlocking the science behind the glass's appearance. In time, everyone forgot what lay inside the glass as its surface dulled and clouded with years.

Till one day, a new scholar appeared at the University, which by now had been built so far that it completely encased the block of glass. He was a young man of modest garb and humble demeanor, but he brought with him a black leather satchel of the kind doctors often carry.

When questioned, he indicated that he wished to study the glass at the University's heart. The other students derided him. By now they had forgotten about the glass, since no study of it had ever yielded the slightest result, and it was regarded a fruitless and outmoded subject. But he persisted, and eventually they took him to the corridor that led to the glass enclosing the mansion's front door.

All he did there was open his satchel. Nothing came from it at all, but after it had been opened for a moment, he smiled and closed it again, before inviting them to go drinking with him.

He and his fellows drank all through the night. And while they did, the tiny clockwork butterflies, too small for the eye to see, that had risen from his suitcase, clung to the glass and slowly ate away at it.

In the morning, the students that had been drinking heard a great crash. The center of the University, an immense airy structure used to study the movements of the stars, had fallen in, lacking the glass upon which its slender struts had once rested.

They rushed to the corridor and found the glass gone. Pressing inside, they found the building, the confused partygoers wandering about among the wreckage covering the garden, the Lord and Lady among them, dressed in antiquated clothes and speaking in accents that had not been heard in a century.

Some pushed on, into the still intact mansion, and wandered its hallways in turn, until they came to a cellar door guarded by a clockwork cat. Inside, the new student sat watching the sleeping Aurora, patiently waiting for her to stir.

Which of course she did. But that story must wait for another tick of the clock, when the angels dance again.

Afternotes:

I wrote this retelling of Sleeping Beauty for a children's project retelling fairytales.

Postscript

I F YOU'VE ENJOYED THESE stories, I hope you'll look for other examples of my work. I write across several genres, but the following list may be helpful.

Eyes Like Sky and Coal and Moonlight was my first fantasy collection. The paper version is out of print, but the electronic is available on Amazon.

Near + Far was my first science fiction collection, published by Hydra House. You can find it in multiple version on Amazon, Smashwords, and Barnes & Noble. A companion volume, *Neither Here Nor There*, appeared in 2016 from Hydra House.

Beasts of Tabat is my first novel, to be followed this year by *Hearts of Tabat*, the first two volumes of the Tabat Quartet. The books appear from Wordfire Press.

If you look at my bibliography on my website at http://www. kittywumpus.net, you'll find links there to many of the stories online.

If you're interested in helping support the production of more stories while getting yourself some good reading, please consider supporting my Patreon campaign.

About the Author

Cat Rambo lives, writes, and teaches atop a hill in West Seattle. Her 200+ fiction publications include stories in *Asimov's*, *Clarkesworld Magazine*, and *The Magazine of Fantasy and Science Fiction* as well as two novels. An Endeavour, Nebula, and World Fantasy Award nominee, she is also the current President of the Science Fiction and Fantasy Writers of America.

www.ingramcontent.com/pod-product-compliance
Lightning Source LLC
Chambersburg PA
CBHW031958010726
47493CB00007B/2253